CIA ASSASSIN

AND OTHER STORIES

Benson Lee Grayson

CIA ASSASSIN

Edward Kramer was sitting in his cubical in the CIA building late one Friday afternoon in mid-June when his phone rang. He picked it up and said "Russian Desk."

"Mr. Kramer?" asked a female voice.

"Yes," he answered.

"Mr. Kramer, can you please come to Mr. Tillman's office right now."

Kramer hung up the phone and stood up. He grabbed his suit jacket from the clothing rack and put it on, carefully straightened his tie, and combed his hair. Walking out of the office into the corridor, Kramer was so happy he had to stop himself from whistling. The phone call was one he was hoping for and expecting. It clearly was in response to the memorandum he had submitted to the Deputy Director three weeks ago requesting that he be permitted to leave the CIA with a full retirement pension.

Kramer knew of no reason why his request should not have been granted. Although he was only forty-eight years of age, he met the Agency's requirement of twenty-five years' of government service for retirement, with twenty-four years with the Agency and two years' of army service. In theory, the CIA could turn him down, but he had never heard of a similar request being rejected.

Waiting impatiently at the elevator, Kramer reviewed in his mind what he should tell Tillman. Would it be better, he wondered, to say he felt burned out and no longer able to perform as well as he should? Or was it preferable to speak the truth, to admit that he still loved his work but was resigning for family reasons? The real reason for his retirement was his desire to regain his ex-wife Barbara. She had divorced him six years ago. At the time she had said that while she still loved him. However, she could no longer put up with his prolonged absences from home. It was too hard for her to try to raise their two children by herself while coping with the knowledge that he was doing dangerous work that might cost him his life.

After a few minutes when the elevator had still not arrived. He impatiently headed to the staircase and walked up the flight to the fifth floor, on which the office of the CIA Deputy Director of Operations was located.

The fifth floor housed the suites of many of the senior officials of the Agency Directorate of Operations, the part of CIA responsible for conducting espionage, sabotage and other clandestine activities abroad. Kramer came to this floor rarely, the last time to attend the retirement party of Tillman's predecessor as Deputy Director. As always, he was struck by the fact that this corridor was so much better decorated than the lower floor corridors, with gold-framed oil paintings and framed antique maps on the walls. Entering the Deputy Director's suite, Kramer gave his name to the reception and waited expectantly as she said something on the intercom. She then directed him to enter the door behind her.

The office was much as he remembered it, large and with thick Oriental carpets on the floor, mahogany bookcases along one wall and a large executive wooden desk facing the door. Two large windows along one wall gave a beautiful view of the surrounding Virginia countryside. There was only one problem. Except for himself, the room was empty. Kramer looked around, wondering if there had been some misunderstanding. He was about to go back to the receptionist when the door opened and a man whom he had never seen before entered.

The newcomer was about forty, slightly taller than Kramer's five feet ten inches, and dressed in an expensive three-piece suit. "Mr. Kramer," he said as he seated himself at the desk, "I am Warren Brewster, Mr. Tillman's Executive Assistant. He asked me to take charge of your request. Won't you please be seated," Brewster continued, directing Kramer to the leather easy chair facing the desk.

Brewster opened the file he was carrying and perused it, as though to make certain he was speaking correctly. Looking up, he said, "I am happy to inform you your request for immediate retirement has been approved, with an effective date of this Friday. I trust this meets with your satisfaction."

Kramer smiled. This was better than he had hoped. No nonsense about waiting until he trained a replacement. "And when do I receive my retirement check?" he asked.

Brewster looked up at him, a surprised expression on his face. "Pension? There is no pension. Since you retired before your fiftieth birthday, you're not eligible for a pension."

"But I served in the army for two years before joining the agency, so I have the required minimum number of years," protested Kramer. "Officers in the Operations Directorate have always been allowed to retire with a pension from the Agency after twenty-five years of government service."

"I'm afraid that's no longer true," Brewster said. "It was true, last year. However, we were instructed by the Finance Office that because of budgetary restraints, no pension can be granted unless an officer is at least fifty. Since you're only forty-eight, you do not qualify for a pension."

"But that's ridiculous!" Kramer protested, "I served my time doing dangerous work."

"That's all true. I wish we could help you, but our hands are tied."

"Why wasn't I informed of the change?" Kramer demanded. "I certainly deserve that. I can't afford to retire without a pension. I withdraw my request for early retirement."

Brewster shrugged his shoulders. "You should have been informed of the change in eligibility. Unfortunately, your request arrived the same day that the change in age took place, and no one thought to notify you about it."

"So I have to wait until I'm fifty to receive my pension?"

"There can be no pension now, or when you turn fifty."

Kramer reddened, his anger rising. "I want to see Mr. Tillman. Please tell him it's urgent."

"It will do you no good," Brewster answered. The directive from Finance was specific on that score. Exemptions can only be granted with the personal approval of Mr. Tillman based on exceptional circumstances. There is nothing about your case which would justify such an endorsement. In any case, Mr. Tillman is out of the country on a mission and unable to see you."

Brewster stood, signaling that the meeting was over. He turned and started to leave, then stopped and faced Kramer. "There may be a way," he said, "If you're willing."

"For God's sake tell me," Kramer begged.

Brewster returned to his chair and motioned Kramer to sit. "everything I'm going to tell you is top secret," he said seriously, "Do you understand?"

"Yes, sir."

"This week," Brewster began, "We discovered a senior officer on the Counter Intelligence Staff, Walter Cooper, has defected from the Agency. He managed to slip over the border into Mexico and has flown to Vienna, Austria where he is negotiating with the Russians. We checked his computer and found out he gained access to all of the files of our agents in Russia and now he is offering to provide all this data to Moscow in return for a large cash payment and the promise of safe-haven in a neutral country."

Kramer listened carefully, wondering what all this had to do with his situation. He was about to ask this of Brewster when the latter explained. "If Cooper carries out his intentions, it will be catastrophic for this country. He has to be stopped, eliminated."

Kramer stared at him, shocked. "What do you mean by eliminated? Surely you're not suggesting the Agency is going to murder him? It's against the law. We can't just kill people we don't like. Particularly not an American citizen."

Brewster smiled. "It's not really murder. It's a judicial execution. Cooper is a traitor. If we were able to get our hands on him, he'd be tried formally and sentenced to death. He certainly deserves to executed for what he will do to the United States. What we need is someone to carry out the sentence."

"But I'm no hit-man. I've never killed anyone, not even when I was in the army."

"Mr. Kramer," Brewster said slowly, "Cooper will be killed. If you choose to take on the job, the Agency will be grateful. You will have done us and your country a great service. If you choose not to, simply get up leave this room and forget this conversation ever took place."

"But what about my pension?" Kramer almost shouted. "That's the reason I came up here. I'm not volunteering to kill anybody."

Standing up, Brewster shrugged his shoulders. "I thought I had made it clear," he said, "That there will be no pension. However, should you eliminate Mr. Cooper, the Agency will be very grateful. In fact, I can assure you that should you carry out that mission for the country, a memo would go that day to the Director, stating that you had performed a service of such inestimable service for the CIA that it was requested you be granted an immediate pension equivalent to what you would have earned after thirty years."

It took a couple of seconds for Kramer to comprehend what Brewster was driving at. "Do you mean to say," he asked, "That if I kill Cooper for you, I get an immediate pension?"

"Not exactly. The CIA cannot kill anyone, particularly an American citizen. It is against the law. However, that would not prevent us from being extremely grateful if Cooper were removed."

Kramer had heard rumors of the Agency circumventing the law through devious procedures but was nonetheless surprised to find himself involved personally in such an enterprise. "But I wouldn't know how to go about such a thing," he said. "Do you really want me to go to Vienna and shoot him? How would I avoid being arrested by the police?"

As he said this, he was shocked by his own words. Was he actually agreeing to murder Cooper in return for a pension? Still, he told himself, it wasn't murder; what was the phrase Brewster had used – legal execution?

Brewster smiled. "No, nothing like that. We certainly wouldn't want you to be arrested. We would furnish you with all the necessary materiel."

"All right. Tell me what I have to do," Kramer said, surrendering to the inevitable.

Brewster went out, returning with a small carton. He opened it and handed Kramer, a small photograph of a man's face. "This is Cooper. It was taken a few months ago. We have no report that he has altered his appearance in any way so you should have no problem in identifying him."

"Cooper," Brewster continued, "Is using the name of Roger Howard. He is at the Carpathian Hotel. It is a small residential hotel in downtown Vienna near the Opera House." Removing a small case from the carton, Brewster opened it and handed it, Kramer. "This," he explained, "Is a kit carried by diabetics when they travel. It contains two vials of insulin and several hypodermic needles. You will take it with you to Vienna."

Kramer looked confused. He was about to tell Brewster he was not diabetic, but the latter explained. "The vials do not contain insulin, but a highly lethal substance developed by the Agency. One drop injected into the bloodstream will cause a person's heart to stop immediately. Within seconds, the target will be dead from what will look like a massive heart attack. No traces of the compound will be detectable."

"It's important for you to remember," Brewster went on, "That the compound must be injected intravenously into the bloodstream. It's harmless on the surface of the skin and if ingested will only make the person ill. When you are about to use it on Cooper, simply fill one of the hypodermics with the contents of a vial and inject it into one of his blood vessels. "

"And how do I persuade Cooper to cooperate and permit a stranger injecting him with a hypodermic?"

Brewster smiled. "That also has been taken care of. The case contains a small bottle of alcohol, which someone taking an insulin shot would use to disinfect his skin before piercing it with a needle. The alcohol has been laced with an anesthetic. One whiff in the vicinity of Cooper's face will cause him to lose consciousness for a few seconds, enough for you to use the hypodermic."

As Kramer sat contemplating the enormity of the project he was about to undertake, Brewster took out a large manila envelope and handed it to Kramer. "This contains cash for your expenses, four thousand dollars. Use it for your airline tickets, hotel costs, etc. It should be more than enough. Just initial this slip for me to use to cover the expenditure," he said giving Kramer and small government receipt form and then putting it in his pocket. There is no need to keep an accounting. If you have any excess, keep it; it is from unvouchered funds."

"Remember," Brewster stressed, "Cooper must be eliminated before he can leave for Russia before h can undergo detailed debriefings there. Once he leaves Vienna alive, our arrangement is off. Do you understand?"

"Kramer nodded. "I do."

"Fortunately, Brewster said," There is no need for you to obtain a visa. The Austrians do not require a tourist visa for American citizens."

"I have my diplomatic passport.

"No, I'm afraid you don't. Your termination is effective at the close of business today. When you leave the building this afternoon, your CIA badge and passport will be picked up. You will have to travel on your tourist passport."

Kramer stared at him. "But I don't have a tourist passport," he said. "'I did have one, but I never bothered to get a replacement. Whenever I traveled, it was on official business, and I used my diplomatic one."

Brewster thought for a minute before answering. "We can handle that. Go down to the basement, to room B143A. They can provide you with a passport. At the same time, they'll give you a medical card identifying you as a diabetic. That will document your need for the case with the vials and needles. One more thing. It's necessary for you to acknowledge reading this form. It's required for all those leaving the Agency. It states you are required by law to avoid disclosing any classified information to any unauthorized person."

The form was a multi-page document. Kramer started to read it and found it was filled with the usual governmental legal terminology. To go through it carefully would require an hour at least.

"It's not necessary for you to sign it." Brewster said. "Just initial the bottom of the last page."

Kramer complied. He knew he ought to read all of it, but he was emotionally exhausted.

Brewster stood. "Good luck then," he said."

Standing up too, Kramer asked," How do I inform you when the job is done so that I can get my pension?"

"There is no need for you to inform anyone. Our Vienna Station will hear of it as soon as the hotel manager informs the Viennese police of Cooper's death. They will notify the Embassy that an American citizen has died, and the Embassy will pass the word to the Station. As for your pension, we will start work on requesting it as soon as we hear from the Station. It may take a few weeks for Finance to handle the paperwork; you should receive your first check at the end of two weeks; say three just to be sure."

As Kramer headed for the door, Brewster wished him good luck. Kramer thanked him, wishing he had never submitted his request for retirement. How could anyone, he asked himself, sincerely wish someone good luck in committing a murder? Only a psychopath. All of his colleagues at the Agency had struck him as normal. He wondered if the senior officials were different. If they were, perhaps it was just as well that he had not moved up to their ranks.

Kramer took the elevator down to the basement and found room B143A tucked in at the end of a long corridor. It was not a part of the basement Kramer had frequented before and seemed devoid of activity. Entering the office, he approached the woman sitting at the desk and gave her his name. "Oh, yes, Mr. Kramer," she answered, "We were told you'd be coming. Do you have any passport photos with you?"

"No, I don't. Will that cause a problem?"

"Not at all. Please follow me."

11

The woman led Kramer into an inner office, asked him to sit down in front of a white screen, and took several photos of him with a large mounted camera. She then gave him a form to fill out asking him to list his name, place and date of birth, height, weight and hair and eye color. When he handed the completed form to her, she told him that it would take approximately an hour for the passport to be processed. Kramer was welcome, she told him, to wait in the office until it was ready or, if he preferred, to come back at that time.

Rather than wait in there, Kramer decided to go back to his office and inform his colleagues of his leaving the Agency. He took the elevator back up to his floor and walked to the office housing the Russian Desk. Many of the desk personnel had already left, hoping to take advantage of the beautiful June day.

Kramer was glad to see that his desk chief Paul Harrigan was still there. "Paul," Kramer told him, I have to tell you this is my last day, they've approved my request to leave the Agency." Kramer stumbled a bit as he said this; searching for a synonym for "retire" and not wanting to use the pejorative word "terminated."

Harrigan looked at him surprised. I heard you had submitted a request in for early retirement. I'm glad they approved it, but I expected they'd allow me time to find a good replacement for you. You've done an excellent job, and you'll be hard to replace."

"It came as a shock to me, too," Kramer said. He thought of going into more detail about the circumstances of his departure but decided against it. Harrigan was a friend, but it would be unwise to go into the meeting he had had with Brewster. "I'm very sorry to leave you in the lurch," Kramer went on. "I expected to stay on for a few weeks more, but they gave me no choice. They picked the date. They made it clear that when I leave here this afternoon, I'm through."

Kramer spent the next half hour briefing the desk chief on the agents he was handling so that Harrigan hopefully would be able to cover for him until someone was assigned to replace him. Looking at his watch, Kramer added a few more detail, then stood. "I've got to leave now," said. They shook hands and Harrigan wished him a pleasant retirement.

Back down in the basement, Kramer returned to B143A to pick up his passport. The woman at the desk looked up as he entered and said, "Good timing. We've just finished work on your passport. She handed it to him along with a card indicating he was a diabetic. He thanked her and took the elevator up to the first floor and headed to the exit.

Passing the guard on duty at the exit, he placed his employee identification badge into the exit gate as required to open the barrier. Instead of opening, the gate emitted a horrendous shrieking sound. The guard rushed over and turned off the alarm. "The machine has rejected your badge," he said, putting his right hand on the butt of his revolver.

"I'm sorry," Kramer apologized. "This is my last day at the Agency. They told me to hand in my badge as I left."

The guard relaxed, removing his hand from the revolver. "What's your name.?"

"Edward Kramer."

The guard removed a notepad from his pocket and checked it. "That's right, Mr. Kramer," he said. He inserted a key into the machine, which released Kramer's badge. The guard pocketed it, then opened the barrier with another key and stood aside, permitting Kramer to leave the building.

Outside, Kramer turned and took a last look at the Agency Headquarters Building. He had worked for the CIA the greater part of his life. There had been many good times and some bad. Now he was leaving it for good. It was not at all as he had expected, no retirement party at which he was honored by friends and colleagues, no award of a medal for good work. Instead, he was off to murder someone. It was hard not to feel sorry for himself. To keep from crying, he cursed under his breath.

Kramer reached his car, which was parked in a space close to the building, one of the benefits of his occupying a senior position on the Russian desk. He drove through the gate protecting the CIA Compound and down the Parkway along the Potomac River to Washington. Traffic was light until he crossed the bridge into Washington where he quickly became entangled in the rush hour traffic.

Traffic eased somewhat as Kramer turned north onto Rock Creek Parkway and drove up to the Q Street exit in Georgetown. Kramer's residence was a furnished efficiency apartment in a small apartment house overlooking the park. It was far less commodious and prestigious than the house he had formerly owned in Georgetown. He had found it too depressing to live there alone in it after his wife and family had left him and had sold it within six months.

Barbara had generously told him to keep the money, but he had insisted on sending her half of the proceeds of the sale, not that much really after the loan he had taken to purchase the house had been deducted. The fact that he was living in an efficiency did not bother him; he spent much of his time away on foreign trips and would have found it difficult to care adequately with his old lawn and garden.

The first thing he did upon entering his apartment was to turn on his computer and look up the schedule of airline flights from Dulles to Vienna. Kramer found that the most convenient flight for him was the direct one from Dulles Airport each evening at six pm. It was already too late for him to make that evening's flight so he made reservations for the next day, leaving the return date to be determined subsequently.

His transportation arranged, Kramer thought it prudent to count the cash that Brewster had furnished him. He counted the bills which were crisp, new condition, though the serial numbers were not in any sequence. To his surprise, he found the sum was more than the four thousand dollars mentioned, amounting to forty-three hundred and twelve dollars. He wondered if Brewster had been mistaken or had added some unmentioned sum for contingencies.

More than four thousand dollars struck Kramer as far too much to be carried in cash abroad. He had paid for his air tickets via his credit card and would use the card for most additional expenses as hotel rooms and meals. Fortunately, he had obtained a relatively high spending limit for his credit card to cover his trips overseas for the Agency. This was a necessary precaution since the CIA routinely expected its operatives to cover such expenses ad put in for reimbursement only upon their return to Headquarters.

Kramer decided that the next day, before leaving for the airport, he would deposit most of the cash in his checking account, taking only some five hundred dollars with him. That sum, he decided, should handle all emergencies.

His preparations almost completed, Kramer made himself a light supper. The efficiency afforded only limited cooking facilities, a refrigerator, an electric hot plate and some shelves in what had been originally intended to be a closet to hold dishes and pans. Dishes had to be washed in the bathroom sink.

Kramer handled his limited cooking facilities by on weekdays eating his breakfast and an early dinner in the Agency cafeteria while he was in Washington and using his home kitchen only on weekends. To handle the frozen dinners he used those days, he purchased a small electric toaster oven which did not require a special power outlet.

The next morning Kramer slept uncharacteristically late. Rather than make breakfast at home, he decided to treat himself to a big breakfast out. He walked to the nearest restaurant open, a dinner, and had a meal sufficient to carry him through to dinner. On the way back to his apartment he stopped off at his bank to deposit most of the cash he had received from Brewster.

Back home, Kramer packed his suitcase for the trip. He preferred to pack light and avoid having to carry a heavy suitcase. If his stay was longer than expected, he could always purchase a new shirt or have his clothing cleaned at the hotel. He also was careful yo find room in the suitcase for the diabetics kit furnished him by Brewster containing the materials to be used in Cooper's assassination.

The taxi he had called picked him up at thee and Kramer arrived at the departure lounge of Dulles Airport shortly before four, in plenty of time to pick up his ticket and go through the security barriers. He took the time after clearing security to stop at a bookstore and purchase a small paperback German-English, English German dictionary. He had been to Vienna twice before on operational missions and once on a vacation there with Barbara and had never found his lack of German a problem. He realized he was subconsciously hoping that by studying German on the flight, he would divert his mind from the awful deed he was about to perpetrate.

Kramer was unsuccessful in upgrading his seat to business class. As usual when he was obliged to fly tourist class, he found the leg room insufficient for comfort and the meals served almost inedible. He managed to sleep for brief periods, diverting his attention in between naps to study German.

Touching down in Vienna a little after nine the next morning, he secured his suitcase and took a taxi to the

Carpathian Hotel. Kramer found that the air line had made the room reservations that he had requested and registered without incident. "Is my friend, Roger Howard checked in yet?" he asked the desk clerk, using the name Brewster had told him Cooper was using as an alias."

The clerk said he had been there for some days and gave his room number as four twenty-nine. Kramer thanked the clerk and followed the bellhop who was carrying his bag up to his own room, a floor above Cooper. After tipping the bellhop, Kramer sat down on the bed and began planning how to get close enough to Cooper to administer the fatal injection.

The easiest way would be to approach Cooper as a fellow American and suggest that they have dinner together. However, Cooper would probably be suspicious and refuse. This left him with the alternative of contacting Cooper in the guise of a hotel employee. Kramer's ability to speak German was not up to the task, so that he would have to put on a convincing performance of an Austrian speaking English.

Kramer had no idea if Cooper was in his hotel room or even in the hotel. He decided to first reconnoiter the hotel corridor in the vicinity of Cooper's room. Leaving his own room, he headed toward the elevators, passing a service closet. It occurred to him that he might find something useful, so he turned back to the service closet. He tried the door handle and found it unlocked.

Kramer looked around to assure himself the corridor was empty, then quickly entered the room, turned on the light and closed the door. He looked around to see if there was anything useful. On a row of hooks hung several work uniforms, with the employees' name on the pocket. Selecting one he found that he could wear it, although the fit would be problematic. There were also several closed tool chests on the floor. He grabbed one, folded the uniform over one arm, and carefully left the closet, remembering to turn off the light.

Back in his room, Kramer changed out of his clothes and put on the uniform. As he feared, it was almost tight enough to make him look ridiculous. He opened his suitcase and removed the diabetic's bag containing the hypodermic needles and the vials labeled insulin containing the lethal solutions. Filling a needle with the contents of one of the vials, he carefully placed it in the tool chest along with the chloroform bottle Brewster had given him.

Kramer too the staircase rather than the elevator down to the fourth floor to lessen the possibility of one of the hotel staff seeing him. He would down the corridor to room 429. No one was in sight. Inside he heard the noise of what appeared to be the audio of a TV set or radio. He knocked and after a few minutes the door opened.

Kramer found himself face to face with a man in his mid forties, slightly taller than he was a considerably heavier. From the photo Brewster had given him, he had no doubt that this was Cooper. Still, he had to be certain.

"Are you Herr Howard?" he asked. His attempt to imitate a German speaker speaking English struck him as ludicrous, much like that of a second-rate vaudeville comedian.

Fortunately, he caught himself just in time to avoid asking if the man was Cooper, which would have given the game away.

"Yes," Cooper answered, "What do you want?" His tone was petulant. He would be a hard man to like, Kramer decided.

"I'm the hotel plumber," Kramer said. "May I come in? There's a leak in the room below you. May I check out your bathroom sink and toilet? It will only take a few minutes."

"If you have to," Cooper agree. About as grudgingly as he could have without refusing. he stepped aside and Kramer walked into the room to the bathroom. Kramer first made a pretense of checking the toilet for a leak. He then knelt down, opened the bathroom cabinet housing the sink and emptied it of its contents, rolls of toilet paper, cleansers and and extra bars of soap.

Opening the tool chest, he removed a wrench and hit one of the pipes to create the impression of his working on it. "Could you come in here please and help me?" he asked, "This valve is stuck and I can't tighten it and hold my flashlight at the same time. I need someone to hold the flashlight for me."

"God damn it" Cooper swore, "Why didn't you bring somebody to help you? I don't work for this damn hotel."

Nonetheless, he came into the bathroom and took the flashlight Kramer gave him. "Here," Kramer said, "Point the flashlight at this joint. "

As Cooper concentrated his attention on shining the beam on the joint, Kramer removed the bottle of chloroform from the tool chest, poured some on a wad of toilet paper, pretended to lubricate the wrench with it and then quickly jammed the wad of toilet paper under Cooper's nose.

Cooper dropped the flashlight, made a gasp, and then felt to the floor, Kramer catching him just in time to prevent Cooper's head from hitting the tile floor. Kramer flushed the chloroform drenched wad into the toilet and flushed it down. Removing the hypodermic needle from the tool chest he considered where to administer the injection. One spot unlikely to be notice and easily accessible without undressing Cooper he decided was the fold between the skin and forefinger of Cooper's right hand. He first removed his work glove to better control the hypodermic and then inserted I and pushed the plunger down as hard as he could. Cooper gasped again, made a rasping sound and stopped breathing. Kramer checked his pulse. There was none. Cooper was obviously dead.

Kramer returned the empty hypodermic to the tool chest, put on his working glove and with considerable effort managed to drag Cooper's corpse out of the bathroom and onto the room carpet. He turned the body over so that Cooper was face down, as though he had fallen to the floor after suffering a massive heart attack.

Returning to the bathroom, Kramer replaced everything he had removed from the cabinet housing the sink. He looked around the room carefully, ensuring that he was leaving it in the same state he had found it. He did the same in the bedroom, carefully stepping around Cooper's corpse. The TV was still blaring away. Kramer thought of turning it off, but decided against it. If the loud noise resulted in complaints and an earlier discovery of the body, so be it.

Kramer carefully opened the room door, determined that the corridor was empty, and carrying his tool chest walked to the staircase and walked up to his own floor. Back in his own room, he doffed the hotel uniform and put on his own clothes. Next, he removed the diabetic's kit and the bottle of chloroform from the tool chest. He opened and emptied into the toilet the unused vial of lethal solution, then washed out both vials and the hypodermic needle before restoring them to their former position in the kit.

Now to ditch the kit. It was clearly not something he could leave in the trash basket in his room. The kit was too large to fit into his jacket pocket and he did not wish to be seen carrying it out of the hotel and returning without it. Concealing it in some tourist literature he found in his room, he walked to the elevator and took it to the lobby.

Kramer walked through the lobby as rapidly as he could, keeping his face averted from the reception desk to avoid the hotel clerk whom he had asked about Cooper seeing him. Outside on the street, he walked for about twenty minutes until he passed a large dumpster, into which he tossed the diabetic's kit contained the needle and vials. Heading back to the hotel, he deposited the tourist literature he had been carrying into a litter can.

He had no idea whether Coopers corpse had been discovered yet. Whether it had or not, the thought of returning to the hotel in which he had murdered a stranger disgusted him.

Kramer was sorely tempted to register in another hotel for the night, but realized that would be foolish. Not only would it be a waste of money, but it might expose him to suspicion of the police tried to question the hotel guests about Cooper's death. He forced himself to return to the hotel. As he strode through the lobby he glanced out of the corner of his eye and was relieved to see the clerk who had registered him was not at the desk.

In his room, Kramer turned on the TV and found an English-language news show he could look at in an attempt to divert his mind. His watch indicated it was almost time for dinner. He had no interest in going through the lobby to eat. He called room-service and ordered them to send p a roast beef sandwich and a bottle of beer. When the waiter had brought it into his room and left, he managed to choke down half of the sandwich without really tasting it. At least the beer was good, cool and refreshing and a bit relaxing.

In part to raise his spirits, Kramer removed from his jacket pocket the United Airlines schedule he had picked up and checked to see how early on the next day he could fly back to Washington. He found that he could take a United flight at 10 am. However, when he called the airline to make the reservation, he found that he couldn't get through. After several futile attempts, he gave up, deciding to get to the airport early and hope to find a seat on the flight available.

Leaving a week-up call with the operator, he watched the TV for a bit and then tried to go to sleep. The image of Cooper's gasping and then dying as he plunged the needle into him kept reappearing in his mind. Finally in desperation he got up and looked into the refrigerator. He found a small bottle of scotch in the section of items for sale, opened it and drank it all. This allowed him to fall into a fitful, troubled sleep.

The next morning Kramer was awakened by the hotel operator's wake-up call. He quickly dressed, packed and went down to the lobby carrying his suitcase. To his relief, the desk clerk who registered him was not there. Kramer stifled the temptation to inquire about Cooper, hurriedly paid his bill, went out side and hailed a taxi to take him to the airport.

At the United Airlines' counter Kramer was told the flight to Washington he wished to take was completely full. Rather than wait for a subsequent flight which would have had several intermediate stops and take much longer, he paid the premium to obtain a first-class seat. The charge was steep, but he couldn't bear to sit around the Vienna Airport.

Passing through security, he purchased a paperback book with a lurid cover to read while waiting to board and on the flight. He considered eating something at the airport, but decided to have just a cup of coffee and depend on the meals served on board. A short time before his flight was scheduled to be called he went to the toilet. While there he recalled the diabetic's card Brewster had given him to justify his carrying the diabetic's case and the vials labeled insulin. He removed the card from his wallet and painstakingly tore it into small pieces, putting some of the fragments in the trash can in the toilet and the others in various trash cans around the airport waiting room. Now he had destroyed the last physical evidence tying him to Brewster and the murder.

When his flight was at last called, Kramer enjoyed he rare luxury of boarding first with the other first-class passengers. His seat in the first-class compartment was far more comfortable than it had been in the tourist class coming over and the additional leg room was very welcome. From now on, he promised himself, if he had to fly it would be in first-class accommodations.

The meal when it was served was tasty. Kramer ate slowly to savor the food. He then read some of his book, stopping to the watch the in-flight movie when it began. A second film and then a second meal contributed to his enjoyment of the flight, and he was in a satisfied frame of mind as his plane touched down in Dulles Airport and he disembarked and took the bus to the terminal.

Traffic on the highway leading from the airport was heavy, so that it was almost diner time before the taxi dropped Kramer at his Georgetown home. He unpacked, think he ought to go to sleep early to be ready to go to work tomorrow. Then the awful realization came that he had been terminated by the Agency and he would never go back to work there again. A whole chapter in his life was definitely over.

``To cheer himself, he decided to call Barbara and break to her the good news that he had retired from the Agency and was planning to come up to Maine to visit her and the children. He would tell her he was planning to take a vacation there; hopefully she would be as happy to see him as he would be to see her and invite her to stay with her. Her dad's home, in which she and the children had lived since she had left him, was really an estate overlooking the Atlantic. Her father, who owned a chain of small Maine newspapers, had several times suggested that he leave the Agency and take up an executive post with the company; he would hint now to her father that he'd like to accept the offer.

The maid who picked up the phone quickly summoned Barbara. "Dearest," He said as she got on the line, "This is Ed. How are you?"

"Ed., Oh? Fine thanks." Her voice was cold, completely devoid of any emotion.

"Honey," he continued. "I wanted to tell you I've retired from the Agency. A compete separation. I thought I'd come up and spend some time getting reacquainted with you and the kids."

"I don't think that's a good idea right now," she answered. "Of course you're welcome to come up and visit with the children. However, I'm seeing someone regularly. Paul Lamont. He's the Chief Finance Officer of Daddy's company. I believe you met him at the party at the country club when we were all here that last Christmas. Bobby is with him on a fishing trip. Lois and I are going to join them tomorrow to go hiking in Canada."

Her voice was as cold and devoid of emotion as the woman announcing departures at Dulles Airport. Every instinct told him that whatever love she might have felt for him once was long since dead. "I see." he said. "Just give them my love. I'll call you again sometime."

Hanging up, he cursed aloud. He should have realized that six years was a long time. He had been incredibly foolish to think he might rekindle their love. If only he hadn't resigned from the Agency. At least then he would have had his work to give meaning to his life.

Kramer had a hard time falling asleep. He thought of taking a drink and even went so far as to get out a bottle of scotch and unscrew the cap before putting it down. It would be too easy to permit his depression to lead him into alcoholism.

The next morning he mentally calculated the amount he had spent on his trip to Vienna. After all expenses, he still had over eleven hundred dollars remaining from the sum Brewster had given him. He decided to give himself a week of vacation at the beach. He packed a small suitcase and drove to Bethany Beach on the Delaware coast. Although the season had started, he was successful in finding a small apartment in a high-rise condo facing the beach.

The weather was perfect and Kramer went to the beach every day. He loved the ocean and relaxed between swims reading and doing crossword puzzles. He loved seafood and generally bought fresh fish at a nearby stand and cooked it on the grill on his apartment balcony. Twice he went into town to a lobster restaurant.

One night after eating out he stopped off at a bar and struck up a conversation with an attractive woman I her late thirties. When he drove her back to her hotel, he was on the brink of asking to spend the night with her, but desisted. He would have enjoyed the sex, but decided she was the sort to seek a more permanent relationship. Kissing her on the cheek, he left her at the door looking perplexed and annoyed.

Kramer left the beach at the end of the week, returning home rested and relaxed. The first thing he did in his apartment was check to see if there was any news about the start of his CIA pension. There was none, but that had to be expected. His experience was that any sort of personnel action at the Agency took a minimum of two weeks to be approved and another week for the processing to be completed.

He decided to use the next two weeks until he might receive his first check by looking into job opportunities. He answered several want ads he found in "The Washington Post" for foreign affairs analysts and he wrote to some dozen schools to see if they had any vacancies for teaching foreign affairs. He stressed that he had earned a master of art's degree in Russian government before joining the Agency and would be particularly interested in teaching that subject.

Kramer received no responses from the want ads he answered. He assumed they were really intended to obtain a portfolio of potential staff a company bidding for a federal contract might list as available to work on it. On private college in Indiana expressed interest in interviewing him for a teaching position. He considered it but decided to decline; the post was as an instructor, he would have been committed to

28

four different course preparations each term, and the salary absurdly low. If he did go into teaching, he decided, he would go to a first class university to earn his doctorate and then seek a teaching job on a tenure track.

After four weeks of anxious waiting Kramer's first retirement check had still not arrived. Meanwhile, he conceived the notion of suggesting to Brewster than he be given his old job on the Russian desk back. After all, he told himself, he was doing excellent work there and his expertise would be hard to replace. He was certain his old boss Paul Harrigan would support his request for re-appointment. His failure to receive check would be a convenient excuse for him to call Brewster and inquire about the delay. While on the phone, he would sound out Brewster about returning to the Agency. He should have a reasonable chance of persuading Brewster; he might even hint they owed him something for his handing the problem in Vienna.

The first problem Kramer faced was reaching Brewster on the phone. He did not possess Brewster's Agency extension. However, he managed to recall that of Tillman, the Director of Operations. Since Brewster was Tillman's Executive Assistant, the two such be available on the same extension. He dialed the Agency number and asked for the extension.

"Extension 1134," said the voice on the other end, adhering to the CIA practice of answering the phone with the extension number rather than with a name.

"Could I speak to Mr. Brewster, please."

"I'm sorry," came back the voice, "There is no one by that name on this extension."

"Then could I speak to Mr. Tillman's Executive Assistant. My name is Ed Kramer. I worked on the Russian desk and know he's on this extension."

"I'm sorry," said the voice, "Mr. Tillman can not pick up on this line." The phone went dead.

"Damn it," Kramer course aloud, wondering how he could reach Brewster. He decided to wait until lunch time and then call back. Hopefully, the secretary he spoke with would be out to lunch and the office phone covered by someone more cooperative.

Kramer was more successful on his second try. When the call was answered with the standard number of the extension, Kramer said number said, "This is Ed Kramer. I was on the Russian Desk. May I speak with Mr. Tillman's Executive Assistant. It's about an important operational matter."

A minute latter a man's voice on the other end said," This is Paul Savel, Mr. Tillman's Executive Assistant. I was told you wished to speak with me about an important operational matter. I suggest rather than discuss this one phone, you come up to my office and tell me about it."

"I wish I could," Kramer answered. "Unfortunately, I'm retired and out of the building. I can't get in to see you."

There was a moment of silence and then Savel said, "Suppose you give me a general idea of what's this is all about."

"Yes, sir. As I said, I was on the Russian Desk. I submitted a request for retirement some six weeks ago. I told to come up to Mr. Tillman's office and informed by a man who identified himself as Walter Brewster than my request for resignation was approved but that due to a change in regulations I would receive no retirement pension. He promised me that if I did something for the Agency I would receive the pension. I carried out the mission. It's this I want to talk to you about."

"I think you'd better come in Mr. Kramer," Savel said."Come in right now. Go to the visitors' entrance and ask for me. I'll send someone down to bring you up to my office."

Hanging up the phone, Kramer went directly to where his car was parked and drove to the Agency along the Potomac River as he had so many times in the past. He told the guard at the gate that he had an appointment to see Mr. Savel and was permitted to enter the CIA Compound. He parked at the front entrance of the building at visitors ' parking and told the guard at the visitors' desk that Mr. Savel was expecting him. A few minutes later a secretary came down to the desk, obtained a visitor' s pass for Kramer and escorted him to the elevator and then to the Deputy Director's office.

Kramer entered the suite and then an inner office. The door shut behind him and he looked around. It was the same office in which he had talked with Brewster. Behind the desk was a man, in his late thirties. It was not Brewster. It was no one Kramer had ever seen before. Most unusual, he was wearing a vest and suit jacket. Although most CIA officers wore suit jackets to work, they customarily hung them up and worked in their shirt sleeves. This Savel was clearly something special.

"Mr. Kramer," Savel identified himself, "I am Paul Savel, Mr. Tillman's Executive Assistant. Please repeat in detail what you said on the phone."

The CIA grapevine had it that only an operations officer of exceptional ability and character would be selected to serve as Executive Assistant to the Deputy Director. Savel certainly seemed to fit the description. His voice was that of a patrician, his pronunciation testifying to his upper class upbringing and education.

Kramer repeated what he had said on the phone that he had been a case officer on the Russian Desk, had submitted a formal request to retire and had been summed to the Deputy Director's office some six weeks ago. There he had met in this very office with a man who identified himself as Walter Brewster, Mr. Tillman's Executive Assistant. Brewster had informed him his request for resignation had been approved, effective that very afternoon, but that owing to a temporary budgetary restriction, he was not eligible for a retirement pension. Finally, Kramer said that he had been promised his pension would be approved if he conducted a special mission for the Agency.

"What precisely was this mission?" Savel demanded.

Kramer hesitated. Brewster had warned him to mention the Vienna mission to anyone. Still, if he refused to do so, he could hardly expected Savel to assist him. He decided to describe the mission on the assumption that Savel would be privy to most of it anyway because of his job.

"So you are stating," Savel repeated after Kramer had finished, "That Brewster told you the Agency had suffered a high-level defection by one Warren Cooper of the Counter-Intelligence Staff, that the Agency wanted you to murder Cooper before he could pass his secrets to Russia, and furnished you with a kit contained a lethal substance to inject into Cooper in return for granting you a pension."

"Yes, sir. That's right.

"And that you carried out this assignment and killed Cooper."

Yes, sir."

"And specifically what is your purpose in telling me this?"

"Because haven't received my pension and when I tried to reach Brewster I've been told there is nobody in this office by that name."

"I see. Just a minute please." Savel arose and left his office for a minute. Then he returned and sat down at his desk, seeming to wait for a few minutes in silence. Then the door entered and two husky men entered and sat down.

"Mr. Kramer," Savel said," These two gentlemen are from security to escort you out of the building. Kramer was stunned. "But what about what I've told you?"

"Mr. Kramer, I don't know how you came up with such a tale or what your motive may be. But your story simply doesn't hold water."

"Everything I've told you is the God's honest truth," Kramer said, standing. The two security men also stood, ready to grab him if he resisted."

Savel simply sat calmly, showing no emotion. "Mr. Kramer," he continued, unperturbed. "After your call, I attempted to verify your story. I ascertained that you had in fact worked on the Russian Desk and that you submitted a written request to retire. Your retirement was approved without prejudice. Due to a temporary financial problem you the Agency was barred from approving retirement pensions to employees under the age of fifty and you were informed of that fact. You elected to retire rather than withdraw your request for a few weeks."

"I was not given an opportunity to withdraw my request. It was simply accepted," Kramer protested.

"If any error was committed in your case, Mr. Kramer, I am sincerely sorry. I can appreciate the fact that you may feel you were unfairly treated. But your story doesn't help you in any way."

"Mr. Savel," It's ll true. Why would I make up a story like that?"

"Mr. Kramer," Savel went on, "I am Mr. Tillman's the Executive Assistant. I've held that position for the past five months. During that period, Mr. Tillman has had no other executive assistants. During that time, there has been no one

34

associated with this office named Brewster. There also has been no defection from the Agency during that time at any level, let alone a high-level one from the Counter-Intelligence Staff. Finally, the Agency, like all parts of the government is banned by law from carrying out an assassination. Any CIA employee who ordered one would be arrested and tried for murder. We are not in the habit of issuing lethal inject kits to anyone.

"I know all that," Kramer almost shrieked. "But that's what happened."

"Do you have any physical proof?" Savel asked. "For example the diabetic's kit?"

"I followed Brewster's instructions and ditched it in a dumpster in Vienna. The same with the card identifying me as a diabetic."

"Mr. Kramer. You are asking me to believe that a non-existent Mr. Brewster in this office ordered you to assassinate a non-existent defector using a non-existent lethal injection kit. And you have not the slightest shred of proof."

"All right," Kramer said. "I admit it sounds crazy. Don't worry. I'm not going to rant or resist. I'll leave. But I swear to you it's all true, every word."

"Mr. Kramer. You seem to sincerely believe what you are saying. If you do, I suggest you visit a psychiatrist and see if he can help you find what's troubling you."

As Kramer walked out of the office, one security man in front of him and one behind, he turned and said over his shoulder," Is there nothing I can do to convince you?"

Startled, Savel said, "You might try and find out who you supposedly killed in Vienna."

Kramer returned to his efficiency in Georgetown in far less an optimistic meed than when he had left it. Savel had practically convinced him that he had made the whole absurd story up. He took out the passport Brewster had given him and examined it. He was relieved to see that he was not delusional and had arrived in Vienna as he had recalled and returned to Dulles on the following day.

How then could he explain what had happened? Savel had given every impression of doing a thorough and fair job in checking out Kramer's story. The only solution Kramer could come up with was that because Cooper's defection was so serious, Tillman had decided not to divulge it to Savel but had handled it himself. Kramer had never met Tillman, but had been in the audience in the CIA auditorium and had heard him making a few comments. He was sure that Brewster was not Tillman.

If Kramer's reasoning was correct, then the thing to do was to speak directly with Tillman. The problem here was how to do so. Kramer knew of no way to contact the Deputy Director by phone and he had no way of entering the building to reach Tillman's office. What he had to do was determine Tillman's home address and talk to him there.

Kramer recalled that the Deputy Director's first name was Amos. He went to his neighboring public library and obtained the phone directories from Washington and from the surrounding areas in which senior CIA officials usually resided. The first thing he determined was that there was no phone number listed for one Amos Tillman. Either Tillman had an unlisted number or the number was listed under his wife's name. If it was an unlisted number he was stumped; he knew of no way a private individual could obtain one of those numbers. The only thing left to him was to hope that the number was listed under Tillman's wife's name.

Kramer painstakingly copied down the numbers belonging to all those listings that might have been Tillman's, seventeen in all. Returning to his home, he began to call them up one by one, in each case asking for Amos Tillman. On the eleventh call he struck pay-dirt. When the woman who answered said that Amos was out walking the dog, Kramer gave her an excuse and hung up. He now knew, or thought he knew the address at which he might find the Deputy Director.

The next afternoon about five, Kramer drove to the address. Tillman lived in a Montgomery County, a Maryland County just across the Potomac from the CIA Headquarters and the home of many senior Agency officials. He was pleased to find it was not in a gated community; Kramer was able to park just a few houses down from the Tillman home.

Kramer had come prepared to wait for some time until Tillman arrived home. He had brought with him a sandwich and soda and a newspaper to read. Whenever he heard a car approach, he put down the paper and carefully watched to see if the car stopped at Tillman'.

Finally, a little after eight pm, a large black luxury car approached and pulled into Tillman's driveway. A man, who could have been Tillman, got out and entered the house. A few minutes later, a woman left the house, holding a small dog by a leash. walking. Kramer considered going to the house and attempting to talk to Tillman there. He decided against it. It would be hard to pressure Tillman to be completely honest with him and there might be adult children or a servant in the house who could assist Tillman to resist if he was inclined to do so.

The following day, Tillman returned to Tillman's house and parked in the same spot as the day before. This time, Tillman arrive home earlier, about seven. A few minutes after entering the house he came out again, walking the same small dog. Kramer got out of his car and followed the Deputy Director.

After following Tillman for about a block, Tillman reached a small grassy area apparently used as a pet are. Kramer walked up to him and said, "Good evening, Amos, your turn to walk the dog?"

Kramer was fairly certain this Tillman was the same man he had seen in the CIA auditorium. He stock his hand into his jacket pocket. He owned no gun, but had a knife sharpener from his kitchen which when clutched in his pocket with his his hand, gave the impression of his holding in it a revolver. "I have a revolver trained on you, Mr. Tillman," he said as threateningly as he could,"Please turn around and walk with your dog back to your house."

"If you want my wallet, take it," Tillman said.

"I don't want your wallet, just shut up and walk ahead. Remember, I have my revolver pointed at you." To emphasize his point, Kramer jabbed Tillman in the back with the end of the knife sharpener.

They walked past Tillman's house to the spot at which Kramer's car was parked. "Stop!" he ordered Tillman as he opened the rear door of his car. "Get in it and take your dog with you1" When the dog resisted, Tillman bent down picked it up and with the dog cradled in his arms climbed into the back seat.

Kramer climbed in next to him and ordered the Deputy Director to put the dog down and put his arms behind his back. Kramer had no handcuffs so he substituted a length of insulated electric wire cord. A Kramer bound Tillman's wrists with the cord the Deputy Director attempted to resist and Kramer was obliged to his him hard on the back of the head to make him stop. Tillman's head fell back and Kramer feared he might have unwittingly injured Tillman seriously.

Tillman groaned and his eyes opened. Kramer breathed a sigh of relief that the Deputy Director did not appear to be seriously injured. To prevent Tillman from crying out for help, Kramer covered his mouth with tape, taking care to ensure that Tillman was able to breath. He then got into the front seat and drove for few blocks until he saw a junior high school. The school appeared dark and deserted; the perfect place to question Tillman unobserved.

Kramer parked, turned off the car lights and got back into the rear seat. Tillman's dog snapped at him and he involuntarily kicked the dog, it omitting a shriek and then whining piteously. Kramer ripped the tape off Tillman's mouth. "I'm sorry to have hurt you," he said, all I want to do is talk to you.

"You have a Hell of a way of talking to people," Tillman spurted out, then caught control of himself and said in a normal voice, " What do you want to talk to me about?"

"My name is Edward Kramer," Kramer began, "I used to work on the Russian Desk."

"So you're the man Paul told me about. You believe you were cheated out of your pension and you'd like me to do something about it. You didn't have to kidnap me. I'll be happy to look into your case."

His tone of voice and facial gestures left Kramer under no illusion that Tillman actually believed him. He was trying to get out of Kramer's clutches and would then inform the police that a dangerous lunatic was on the lose.

"Mr. Tillman," Kramer interrupted. "Please don't patronize me. I have dealt with enough agents to know when someone is lying. Didn't Mr. Savel tell you what I said about seeing a Mr. Brewster, who said he was your Executive Assistant, and who promised I would receive my pension if I murdered a defector from the Agency?"

"He did say something about that."

"Mr. Tillman," Kramer said, "Would anyone make up a story as crazy as that. I swear to you that it's all true. I decided the only reason Mr. Savel didn't know about it was that the defection was so serious you decided to handle it yourself, cutting him out of it."

"Well, it was something like that."

Kramer saw the Deputy Director still didn't believe a word he said. He had to try another tack. "Sir, let's for the sake of argument say everything I've told you is true. Let's also say that everything Mr. Savel told me about its being impossible is also true. Assuming both scenarios are correct, how can we explain the differences?"

Tillman was silent, apparently seriously considering the question. "You know" he said, I think I have an idea. What day did you see Brewster?"

"It was on a Friday afternoon six weeks ago."

"No wonder I knew nothing about your case until Paul briefed me on it. I was away at the North Carolina beach with my family that week and the previous week. And I believe Paul took several days off as well while I was gone. He told me the first thing he heard about your case was when you came to see him to complain you had not received your pension in return for murdering someone in Vienna."

"Who would be in charge if you and Mr. Savel were away?" Kramer inquired.

"Why that would be my deputy, Bob Cameron, but I can't see him involved in anything like this. And there would be no reason for him to order an assassination; as Paul told you, there were no defections."

"Believe me, I will thoroughly investigate your story tomorrow first thing. I'd like you to come to Headquarters tomorrow and have a look at Bob. You can tell me if he's the Mr. Brewster who talked to you. If he is, we'll find out what's going on. If not, we can go from there."

Kramer was uncertain how to respond. It seemed to him that Tillman was being sincere. "All right, he said. I'll trust you." He untied Tillman's hands. "You know, he said, I'm betting my life on you. Please don't let me down."

Tillman turned around. "Would you feel better spending the night at my house. We have an extra bedroom. You can go in with me tomorrow to the office."

"Very much," Kramer answered. "As you can imagine, I'm dead tired from all the recent strain."

Kramer followed the Deputy Director inside the house. "Honey," Tillman called out, "I'm back. I have a friend with me."

Mrs. Tillman came into the room. She was a pleasant-looking woman, about Tillman's age. "Liz," Tillman said, "I'd like you to meet Mr. Kramer. I invited him to spend the night here so he can go in with me to the office tomorrow."

"Glad to meet you Mr. Kramer," she said. Can I get you a cup of coffee?"

Then she saw the blood on her husband's head and said, "Amos, your head is bleeding."

"I fell while walking the dog. Mr. Kramer helped me get up. I'll go up to the bathroom to put a bandage on it. It doesn't seem to be serious."

"Let me show you to your room," Mrs. Tillman said. She led him upstairs to a large bedroom. "It's not really a guest bedroom. It was our son's. He decided a few months ago he wanted to use the bedroom we have downstairs off the rec room so that he can play his music at night without disturbing the rest of the family. You know how teenage boys are."

"Yes, I do," Kramer said, sorry that he was not speaking the truth.

"You don't have any pajamas," Mrs Tillman noted "Let me get a pair of my husband's for you to use."

Kramer was about to tell her not to bother, but she had already gone, returning in a few minutes with a pair.

"This very kind of you, mam. I'm very grateful."

She bid him goodnight and departed. He considered watching television on the small set on a time, but he felt exhausted. He took off his jacket and pants, and hung them up carefully in the closet. Putting on the borrowed pajamas, he lay down and fell into a deep sleep.

Kramer was awakened the next morning by pounding on his door and a male voice saying, "Get up Mr. Kramer. Mom says if you want breakfast you have to get dressed and get down quickly if you want to go into the office with him".

Rather than taking time to shave, Kramer hurriedly dressed, although he did stop to make up the bed he had used so that Mrs. Tillman would not have to do so. Downstairs in the kitchen, he found Tillman just finishing his breakfast while reading "The Washington Post." Tillman looked up say good morning, then returned to read the paper.

"Can I get you some breakfast?" Mrs. Tillman asked him. "We eat a light one, but I can give you some orange juice and a cup of coffee. If you'd like something heavier, I have some cold ham in the refrigerator."

"Just the juice and coffee," Kramer answered, "That would be wonderful."

The Tillmans' son Richie finished the last of a glass of milk, stood abruptly, grabbed his books, yelled "Got to go now, I'm late," and headed out the door." Lois, the Tillman's daughter, was staring at a book instead of eating. When her mother urged her to eat, she said "I can't. I've got a spelling test today and I can't remember these words."

Mrs. Tillman handed Kramer his juice and coffee and sat down next to Lois. "Can I help you, Dear?" she said. "Spelling is really easy."

"Not for me it isn't. Why can't they spell words the way the sound? Shouldn't sugar be spelled with an sh ?"

Kramer laughed. "I had trouble with that word too," he told Lois. "Eventually you get it."

There was a knock at the door. Tillman stood up. "That's my car," he told Kramer. "We'd better go.," He picked up a briefcase with a combination lock, kissed his wife goodbye, wished Lois luck on her spelling test and went to the door, followed by Kramer.

A driver was holding open the rear door of what looked like the same car that had brought Tillman home the previous day. Tillman climbed in followed by Kramer. As the driver cot in and they started off Tillman said, "If you'll pardon me, I have to finish reading some papers before I get to my office. He turned on a small lamp mounted on the rear seat, unlocked he briefcase and began reading a pile of papers. Kramer glanced at them out of the corner of his eye and saw they were all marked "TOP SECRET."

Kramer enjoyed looking out at the scenery as the car sped south along the Potomac River. As a passenger it was much easier to appreciate the view than if he had been driving. Tillman finished his reading just as the car entered the CIA compound. The guards at the gate, apparently recognizing the car, waved it through with out halting it to inspect the occupants. The car drove into the underground garage beneath the Headquarters building and pulled up in front of an elevator.

Kramer got out of the car followed by Tillman, who used a numbered code-board to summon the elevator. The elevator stopped at the first floor and Tillman inserted his badge in the turn-style . After gaining admittance he obtained a visitor's badge for Kramer and then two of them took an elevator to the fifth floor.

Entering the suite housing the Deputy Director's office, Tillman said good morning to the secretary working in it and asked , " Is Mr. Cameron in yet?"

"No, sir."

"Please ask him to step into my office as soon as he arrives."

"yes, sir."

Tillman led Kramer into his office. "Please sit down, " he said. "Bob should be here in a few minutes. Help yourself to one of the newspapers."

Tillman was going through the documents in his in-box when the door to his office opened and a man came in. "You wanted to see me, Amos?" he inquired.

"Yes, it's about that proposal to make a recruitment pitch the Pakistan Desk sent up. I think we need a longer period of assessing the subject to make sure he's really interested in working for us. We don't want to end of with a double agent."

"I agree, I had some doubts about that, too."

"Oh Bob," Tillman said, turning toward Kramer. I'd like you to meet Ed Kramer. He's giving me some information on an operation we had going in Vienna. Ed, this is Bob Cameron, the Assistant Deputy Director of Operations."

Cameron looked startled for a minute, then recovered, saying, "Glad to meet you. Ed," he said. Turning to Tillman, he continued, "I'll send that proposal back to the Pakistan Desk," and left.

"I gather that was not Brewster?" Tillman asked Kramer.

"No, I never saw that man before."

Tillman then picked up his phone and asked the secretary to send Paul in. Savel appeared and stared at Kramer when he saw him. Tillman said, " I just told Bob to send that proposal from the Pakistan Desk back to them with instructions to assess him further. And I believe you know Ed Kramer."

"I've talked to him. I told you about that."

"I remember. He's raised a couple of points I think require a little further checking. I'll fill you in later."

When Savel left, Tillman said, "I gather that was the Savel you spoke to six weeks ago."

Kramer nodded. "Yes, that's the Mr. Savel I spoke to.:

"Good," Tillman said. "So we've established that Bob Cameroon is not Brewster and Paul is the one you spoke with. Now please tell me everything that happened to you in detail since your you were called and told to come to this office."

Kramer did so, with the Deputy Director taking copious notes and stopping him occasionally to elaborate on some points. Tillman was specially interested in the money Brewster had furnished him for expenses, inquiring whether Kramer had any of the bills in his possession. When Kramer answered that none of the original bills was still in his possession, the Deputy Director expressed disappointment. "We might have been able to trace the serial numbers," Tillman said. "But no matter, four thousand dollars is a big enough sum so that I ought to be able to find some record of it, even it came from unvouchered funds".

Tillman also stopped Kramer as he was describing Brewster arranging for him to receive a passport to use in traveling to Vienna. "Was it an American one?" he inquired.

"Yes, an American tourist passport."

"That's most unusual," he commented."The Cover Staff often prepares foreign false passports," But I can't recall many instances of them preparing an American passport of any kind. I'll look into that There will have to be some record."

When the Deputy Director concluded he had extracted everything he could which would aid him in investigating Kramer's account, he put down his pencil and closed the pad in which he was making notes. "Thank you," he said gravely, "For bringing this to my attention. I will personally do everything possible to check it out. In the very least, I will find out why you were not given the opportunity to withdraw your resignation request when the regulations had been changed and you would lose all retirement rights. I should be able to get back to you within a week. If it unexpectedly takes longer, I'll call you at home to give you an interim report."

Kramer concluded this was about as well an outcome as he could reasonably expect. Tillman certainly ought to be able to determine who authorized his tourist passport and from there establish who Brewster was. "I am very grateful at your listening to me and looking into my situation."

"I assume you have no easy way of getting home," Tillman said. "I'll arrange for the motor pool to drive you." He asked his secretary to have someone escort Kramer down to the visitors' entrance. Kramer thanked Tillman again and left with one of the secretaries, who took him downstairs to the exit barrier. . As he stood outside the building waiting for the car to take him home, he felt more cheerful than he had for the past six weeks.

For the next week Kramer waited impatiently to hear from Tillman. When the seventh day passed without a call, Kramer stifled his growing anxiety, telling himself that the Deputy Director had meant seven working days and that he should not count the intervening Saturday and Sunday. On the ninth day after talking to Tillman, Kramer learned the reason for Tillman's silence.

No longer able to read the daily newspapers at the office, Kramer had taken a one month trial subscription to "The Washington Post." In the middle of an inside page he saw a photo that attracted his attention. There was no doubt; it was Amos Tillman. The story beneath it reported the demise of the CIA Deputy Director of Operations Amos D. Tillman. Cause of death was stated to be a heart attack. The address given was that of the house he knew to be Tillman's residence and the name of the widow was Elizabeth.

Kramer's first thought was a selfish one: he would never receive his pension or learn why he had been blackmailed into murdering Cooper. He then realized how unlikely it was that

Tillman had actually died from natural causes; probably someone had given him a lethal injection. The unknown Brewster had acted again, but who was Brewster?

Kramer's first impulse was to call Savel and try and find out what in anything Tillman had told him of the results of his investigation. When called Savel's number, he was told that "Mr. Savel has been transferred to a new assignment abroad."

"May I speak with the Deputy Director then, please," he pressed further.

"I'm sorry," came the response, "Mr. Cameroon can't pick up on this line."

Kramer congratulated himself. At least, he had learned who the new Deputy Director was. So Cameron had benefited from Tillman's death by moving up to his post. And to Kramer, Cameroon's reaction on seeing him had seemed suspicious. But Cameron was definitely not the Brewster he had met with. Who then was Brewster and what was the connection between Brewster and Cameron? He hadn't a clue.

Kramer suddenly recalled the last thing Savel had said to him: "Try to find out the identity of the man you supposedly killed in Vienna." This was easier said than done. The death of a visiting American from an apparent heart attack in a Vienna hotel would not attract much attention in the Vienna newspapers.

If he could not determine who had orchestrated the murder in Vienna, possibly he could unravel the puzzle by finding the motive. The person in charge was obviously some senior Agency official who had access to his resignation

50

request and the power to authorize the Cover Staff to prepare of the tourist passport he used. Why would a senior Agency official organize the murder of an American in Vienna?

Three possible motives came to mind. The first, eliminating a dangerous defector, he quickly ruled out; both Tillman and Savel had stated flatly there had been no such defection. The second motive, to kill someone for a personal reason like jealous or hatred, was possible but not likely. Kramer couldn't visualize any senior Agency official resorting to murder for such a reason and in any case, it would be impossible for him to get any knowledge on such a subject.

Kramer decided that the motivation behind Cooper's murder had to be financial. The Agency routinely expended large sums of unvouchered funds for operational reasons such as covert payments to agents, concealed payments for foreign leaders and parties and arms purchases. It was quite possible that the man he murdered in Vienna, Cooper, was involved in the embezzlement of Agency funds or had somehow learned of such an activity.

If this assumption was correct, Cooper was probably in the CIA Office of Finance. If Kramer were still in the Agency or had any contacts in the Finance Division, it would have been easy for him to determine if anyone in that office had recently died of a heart attack while in Vienna. Unfortunately, Kramer no longer had access to the Headquarters or a contact in the Finance Division.

There was one other avenue of approach he might use. He had never heard of any Finance division staffers being assigned outside of Headquarters. Therefor Cooper was probably a native of the Washington area and his death might have been noted in one of the Washington area papers.

Kramer got up immediately and drove to the local public library. Recent editions of "The Washington Post" were still available and he was able to have librarian bring him copies of the paper for the two weeks after his return from Vienna. Carefully he went through them, starting with the earliest date.

In no paper was he able to find any obituary notice for someone named Walter Cooper, nor for a Roger Howard, the name Cooper was registered under in the hotel. Kramer was about to give up, when he had another thought. Suppose the name of the man he killed was actually not Cooper or Howard, but something else. He went back through the papers to see if he could find someone of the approximate age of the man he had killed, someone in his late forties.

He found three who met the bill with regard to age. He wrote down the names, then checked them in the local telephone directories. One, Thomas Yoder, lived in Montgomery County, Maryland, not too many miles from where Tillman's residence had been located. Kramer decided to drive there immediately to see if he could find out if Yoder was Walter Cooper.

The houses on the street on which the Yoder house was located were not as large and expensive as Tillman's. All were brick split-level homes, looking as the sort that might be occupied by a middle-level official in the Finance Division.

Kramer parked in front of the Yoder house and sat for a few minutes, planning his strategy.

Kramer walked up to the door and rang the door bell. A minute later the door opened and Kramer found himself staring into the face of an attractive woman about his own age. "Mrs. Yoder," he said, "My name is Edward Kramer. I'm with the CIA. He took out his driver's license to confirm his identity. I have a few questions about your late husband. May I come in?"

She looked blankly at home, uncertain. "It will only take a few minutes, Mrs. Yoder, please."

Mrs. Yoder stepped back and opened the door. He entered and followed her into the living room, where they both at down. "Shouldn't you have some sort of identification from the CIA ?" she asked.

"No, not any more. I'm no longer active. I retired six weeks ago."

"Could you please explain what all this is about" she said coolly. "I'm busy right now."

` "Of course," Kramer said reassuringly. "But first I must make sure that you are the right Mrs. Yoder. Do you have a recent picture of your husband I can look at?"

She rose and returned with a photo in a frame. There was no doubt .Thomas Yoder was the man he had killed in Vienna. "Mrs. Yoder," he asked, "Was your husband in the CIA?"

"Yes, there's no secret about that. He was not under cover."

"And did you work for the Finance Division?"

"Yes, what difference does that make?"

"Mrs. Yoder," Kramer said softly. "Your husband did not die of a heart attack. I killed him with a lethal injection."

She jumped up. You're insane," she said. "I'm calling the police."

"Please, Mrs. Yoder. It's all true. I didn't know your husband. I was told he was a traitor on the Counter-Intelligence Staff and was about to turnover vital CIA secrets to the Russians. I was given the lethal injection by a man in the office of the Deputy Director who told me his name was Brewster and that he was the Deputy Director's Executive Assistant."

She sat down. "That's all crazy. Whatever else my husband was, he was no traitor."

" I know that now," Kramer answered. "I was set up. When I came back to Washington I found that no one in the Agency had authorized the murder and that there was no defection."

"I really can't believe anything you've said," Mrs. Kramer told him. "I think you'd better go."

Mrs. Yoder," Kramer pleaded. "Please hear me out. If my assumptions re correct, you're in serious danger. I believe your husband either was involved in embezzling cash from the

Agency or learned of such a scheme. He was murdered either to get the cash or to keep the secret from coming out. I was merely the unwilling puppet who carried out the killing. If the people in charge don't have their hands on the cash, I believe they will grab and torture you to learn if you know where it is."

She shook her head. "Do you have any proof?"

"Did you remember reading in the papers about the death of Amos Tillman, the CIA Deputy Director of Operations?" he asked.

"I think I recall something like that."

"We can look it up in the library if you like. The obituary said he died of a heart attack. I told him what I've just told you and he was supposed to call me back with what he had learned. I think he was killed with the same kind of lethal injection I gave to your husband."

"Why are you telling me all this? Why don't you go to the police?"

"They wouldn't believe me," he admitted. "I was hoping you'd be able to help me obtain some proof. You already have by confirming my assumption that he was in the Finance Division Tell me," he went on, "Did your husband travel much out of the country."

"This last one was only the second; he traveled to Europe for the first time about two months earlier."

"Did he say anything about these trips, where he was going, what he was doing?"

"Tom rarely talked about his work. Actually, we weren't too close for the past few years. " She thought for a minute. "I believe he said something about the weather in Switzerland when he returned from the first trip."

"That could be important," Kramer said. "Switzerland is well-known for the numbered bank accounts available in Swiss banks. A numbered account would be a convenient place to stash embezzled funds. I wonder if he went first to Switzerland on the latest trip. If we looked at his passport, it would indicate whether he visited any other country before Austria."

"I don't have his passport. It wasn't returned with his effects. I never thought to ask about it."

"Someone who knew he was traveling under a false passport in the name of Howard probably intercepted it. "

"Who did you speaking with in the Agency when his effects were given to you?" Kramer asked.

"I'm not sure. I believe his name a Scottish one."

"Cameron?"

"Yes," she said, "It was Cameron. Do you know him?"

"He moved up to become Deputy Director for Operations to replace Till man. I had an idea he behaved queerly when he saw me talking to Mr. Tillman."

"You mentioned a Mr. Brewster who you said told you to kill my husband. Where does he fit in?"

"My guess," he answered, "Is that Brewster works for Cameron. Any operation as detailed as the one involving me and your husband would require a gang rather than being the work of one man."

"I was thinking," Mrs. Yoder said thoughtfully, "You don't have any hard evidence that Tom was involved in any embezzlement. He might have been sent to Vienna to investigate for the Agency."

"That's true," Kramer agreed, deciding to keep his suspicions to himself. "Why don't we look through his papers? Perhaps we can find something that will show his innocence."

She rose and invited him to follow her into an adjoining room. "Tom used this as his office," she said. "I have been trying to organize his things but, as you can see, haven't made much progress."

The first thing that struck Kramer about the room was the large number of business periodicals and stock market letters piled on a desk. "Did your husband play the stock market?" he inquired.

"No. When I asked him about all the stock market stuff he said it helped him on the job in the Finance Division."

Kramer said nothing, but her comment heightened his suspicions about Tom Yoder. As far as he knew, the Finance Division's activities did not include any dealings in the stock market' these were handled by other parts of the agency. Pulling open one of the desk drawers, she said, "Tom kept his monthly bank statements here. Would you like to look at them?"

Kramer looked through the first half-dozen statements. He saw that Yoder maintained a balance in his checking account of roughly a thousand dollars, about what you might expect for someone at his level in the Agency owning a home in his neighborhood. Everything seemed routine and he was replacing the bank statements when he noticed a key in the corner of the drawer. He took it out and examined it. "Isn't this the key to a safe deposit box?" he asked.

"Why, yes."

"Were you aware of this?"

"Certainly. We've had the box for the last four or five years. I have access to it, too, although I haven't visited it since we opened it."

"Do you have an idea of what's in it?" Kramer inquired.

"Mainly important papers. The deed to our house, the title registration for our cars, our birth certificates. Oh, yes, and the passport I used when I traveled to Europe before I was married and my mother's old engagement ring. I was always planning to have it fixed so that I could wear it." She looked wistfully at her left hand, adorned only by a simple gold wedding ring.

"Could we go tomorrow and check the box?" he asked. "There might be something useful in it."

"I have to work," she answered. "There's a meeting I have to go to. But I could go with you at two."

"Great," he said. "I'll pick you up here at two tomorrow." He thanked her and she escorted him to the door. As he said goodnight and walked to his car, he puzzled over what he had learned by speaking to her. A lot of interesting facts, he decided, but nothing conclusive. He was still as much at sea as before.

The following afternoon, Kramer pulled in front of Mrs. Yoder's house and found her waiting outside for him. "I hope I haven't kept you waiting long," he said.

"No, I arrived back from school just a few minutes ago."

"At school?"

"Yes, I'm a librarian at the local junior high."

He followed her directions and parked in the lot of a nearby bank. Inside,, she signed in at the safe deposit desk and gave the clerk her key. They followed as the clerk unlocked the box, handed it to Mrs. Yoder and led them into a small room in which they could open the box. It was crowded, scarcely room for both of them to sit next to the desk on which Mrs. Yoder placed the box. She opened it and emitted a gasp.

Kramer leaned over her to get a better view and saw what had surprised her, Most of the box was filled with bundles of currency. Kramer picked up one and examined it. It contained hundred dollar US bills. Kramer counted and found there were a hundred bills, for a total of ten thousand dollars per bundle. There were four bundles in all, a total of forty thousand dollars.

"God," she said. "I've never seen so much cash in one place in my life. I never knew it was here. Does that mean Tom embezzled this? Is this the reason why he was killed?"

Kramer thought for a minute. "No," he said, "It's not proof he embezzled anything. For instance, he might have made it on the stock market or by gambling, although it is unlikely. I don't think this forty thousand is the reason he was murdered. It's a lot of money, but not a large enough sum to warrant the detailed planning and operation in which he and probably Tillman were killed, I think that this money is only part of what was embezzled, kept here as emergency cash. I would imagine the total amount would have to be at least half a million. Probably not more than two million; it would be hard to embezzle more than that without being caught."

"What do you think we ought to do with it?" she asked.

"I don't like to give advice," he answered, "But if I were you, I'd take those bills and put them in your purse. I'd close up the box and return it, then I'd drive you to another bank where you would open a safe deposit box in your name and put the cash in it."

"Why not just leave it here?"

"Because your husband's name is on it. It would be too easy for the people who orchestrated his murder to locate it and obtain access to the cash, either by stealing the key from you or breaking in surreptitiously."

She started to put the bundles of cash into her purse and stopped. "Look here," she said. "Here's Tom's passport. How

60

did it get here? He had it with him when he went off and it wasn't returned with his effects."

Kramer asked for the passport and examined it closely. It was made out to Thomas Yoder and was a tourist passport. "He didn't use this passport," Kramer said, "When he registered at the hotel in Vienna. He was listed there under the name of Roger Howard."

A slip of paper fell out of the passport. Kramer picked it up and examined it. On top was the hand-written inscription "HDR Bank Zurich AG" and beneath that a six-figured number. "Is that your husband's handwriting?" he asked her.

"It appears to be. Is that a telephone number on the lower line?"

"No, I think that its the number of a number bank account in this Zurich bank." He looked at the passport again. "Yes, this passport stamp shows your husband traveled to Zurich when he made his first trip abroad. He probably also used it to open the numbered account there."

"This means he was involved in the embezzlement?"

"I'm afraid so." Kramer said, as he inserted the slip of paper into the passport and carefully put the passport in his jacket pocket. He got up as Mrs. Yoder put the last bundle of cash into her purse, zipped it shut and handed the closed box to Kramer. They left the room and returned the box and key to the attendant.

Back in his car, Kramer started off, following Mrs. Yoder's directions to a nearby bank. He was surprised when she suddenly told him to pull over to the curb and stop. "Mr. Kramer," she began, then stopped. "This is silly," she said, "Calling you Mr. Kramer. "What's your first name?"

"Ed."

"Ed, mine is Amy." Grinning, he stuck out his hand to shake hers. "The pleasure is all mine, Amy."

"Ed," she continued, "What should we do with the money?"

"You should keep it. I don't know who we could return it to. There's nobody in the Agency I can trust. And if we turned it in to the police, they'd think we were involved in something illegal. There's something else," he added. "I'm afraid I've placed you in deadly peril. The people who had me kill your husband almost certainly know about the rest of the money hidden somewhere. They are likely to grab and torture you to find out where it is and then kill you."

"What do you think we ought to do?"

"We don't have any really good choices." he answered. "Basically, we can either run or fight. If we run, we go as far away from Washington as possible and take on false identities. I know how to do this, but it isn't easy without the Agency's support. It would be hard to live, since we would lose our credentials. You couldn't use your experience as a librarian and I couldn't use my graduate degree to teach. All we'd have would be the forty thousand dollars and that wouldn't take us very far. And we'd always have to be looking over our shoulder to make sure Brewster and his friends wasn't tracking us down."

"That isn't a very attractive prospect. What about the fight alternative? "

"We use the forty thousand to pay our way to Zurich. Using your husband's passport, I we go to the Zurich Bank and withdraw the money from his numbered account."

"Do you think we can get away with that?"

"I am about the same age as your husband. If dye my hair to match his and wear eyeglasses, the odds are the bank won't suspect anything."

"Let's do it then," she said.

"you understand, that is also dangerous. The people who killed your husband probably are watching the Swiss banks and are likely to try and kill us and take the money as soon as we leave the bank. I'm pretty good, but it would be hard for me to protect you from their assassins."

"Is there nothing we can do?" she asked.

"There is one way. Kill who ever is running the operation in the Agency. I believe it is Cameron. I can try to get proof he is the one and then eliminate him However, I can't talk to him without his realizing we have identified him. This will guarantee he goes after us, even if he had no intention of doing so before."

"You mean kill him in cold blood? I don't think I could be any party to that."

"Believe me, I don't want to kill anyone," he told her. "But if it turns out Cameron is the one who had me kill your husband, he deserves to be punished. And, of course, it would really be self-defense. If we don't kill him, he will kill us."

"Promise me you won't act unless you talk to me first."

He saw she was serious. "I promise," he said. "I'll talk to him, and then tell you what I've learned. We'll decide on what to do from there."

Kramer started the car again and followed Mrs. Yoder's directions to the bank she had selected. Inside, he stood by her as she filled out the forms to rent a safety deposit box. When she asked him if he wished to add his name to the box he answered, no. saying it would increase the risk to her.

The bank attendant led them to the room in which they could open the box in privacy. Kramer noted that this room was larger than the room in the previous bank. As she started to put the bundles of cash into the box, Kramer said, "Amy, I suggest you take five or six bills and put them in your wallet. It may be helpful to have some cash available at home."

"That's a good idea. Why not more?" she asked.

"Because if anyone found too much cash in your home, it would raise suspicions. Five or six hundred is a more reasonable amount given your family income."

They waited while the attendant locked the box and gave Mrs. Yoder the key. As they drove back to her house, he cautioned, "Amy, remember to hide the key well. Remember how easily we found the key to your husband's box in his desk drawer."

"Do you have any suggestions?"

You could hide it in a large container of flour or sugar in your kitchen. Even better would be to bake some muffins and put the key inside one. You'd have to mark the one with the key by putting a blueberry or some other edible thing on food to distinguish it. Then put the muffin with the key your refrigerator freezer and eat or throw out the other muffins. They cash I'd conceal in some book you don't use often, say a cookbook, and put the book on a low shelf of the bookcase."

"They sure teach you interesting things in the Agency," she said laughing.

"That they do," he agreed.

"Sit tight," he said, "As the car pulled up in front of her house. "I'll contact Cameron and let you know what learn."

She leaned over and kissed him on the cheek. "I don't know what I'd do without you," she said, getting out of the car. He stared at her, surprised. She was a most attractive woman, he thought to himself, as he drove off.

The next morning about ten, Kramer called the Agency number he had used to reach Paul Savel. "Could I speak to Mr. Cameron?" he told the secretary who answered his call.

"There is no Mr. Cameron available on this extension," came back the expected reply.

"I am aware this is the extension for Mr. Cameron's Executive Assistant," Kramer said. "Please give Mr. Cameron the message that Edward Cooper is on the line and must speak with him on an urgent operational matter. It concerns the link between the death of Thomas Yoder in Vienna and that of Mr. Tillman."

"Just a minute please." Then a man's voice come on the line. "This is Robert Cameron. You should not be revealing any operational matters on this open line, Mr. Kramer. Please come to my office at one this afternoon and we can discus it privately."

Cameron's reaction bolstered Kramer belief that the Deputy Director was fully aware of who Kramer was and had masterminded both Yoder and that of Tillman. The time he was setting for Kramer to come to his office, one pm, was a time the office would be emptied by the staff going to lunch and provide a convenient opportunity for Kramer to be given a lethal injection.

"I'm afraid I can't make it today," Kramer answered. "Why don't we make it at ten tomorrow morning>"

"Fine," Kramer said. "Let's make it for then."

As tempting as it would be to confront the Deputy Director in his own office, Kramer recognized the foolhardiness of placing himself in Cameron's clutches. He devoted the next couple of hours to considering how he might most safely kill Cameron. Kramer was no trained assassin; Yoder was the only person he had ever killed and he didn't even possess a gun.

Kramer's first thought was to see if he could purchase a gun at a gun show from a private dealer, avoiding the need to go through a background check. He checked on his computer, but found the requirements varied by state and that in any case he might have to wait a week or more for the next gun show. His concentration was disturbed by the nagging doubt that Cameron was not involved and that he might be killing an innocent man.

After several hours of fruitless effort, Kramer put the task aside to eat, taking a frozen dinner out of his refrigerator. He was waiting fr the meal to be ready when he heard a loud knock at his apartment door. Kramer was about to open the door when some instinctive caution led him to ask who it was.

The response, "Mr. Kramer, this is the building plumber. We have a leak. I need to check your bathroom."

Something about this was terribly wrong. Kramer had never heard that his building had a plumber. Then he remembered, this was the pretext he had used to gain admittance into Yoder's hotel room in Vienna.

"I'm taking a bath right now. Please come back in twenty minutes."

"It's necessary to do it right now before the water damage gets worse. It will only take a minute."

Kramer quickly locked the chain lock on the door and walked to his phone. Calling the building desk, he asked the clerk if there was a leak in the building. "No, Mr. Kramer," came the answer. The alleged plumber had to be an assassin sent by Cameron to eliminate him. He listened at the door; all was silent. Quietly unlocking the door he peered out into the corridor. Around the corner he saw a slight movement. Someone was hiding there, ready to pounce on him should he venture to leave his apartment.

Kramer briefly considered calling the police and telling them someone was trying to kill him. On reflection, he realized this would be foolish. Even if the police apprehended the assassin, which was unlikely, there would be no proof. He could not tell them t he reason why someone wanted to kill him without revealing the fact that he had murdered Yoder. The most likely result would e that he himself would be taken into custody.

Obviously, the best course was to flee. But how? The assassin was waiting for him outside. Kramer had been trained in hand-to hand combat while in the army, but his skills were rusty. More important, all it would take to kill him would be one scratch on his skin from a lethal filled hypodermic.

He walked over to the window and looked down. His apartment was on the first floor of the building. However, the courtyard below was some twenty feet below because of the above-grounds basement floor, He could jump, but would risk serious danger of breaking an ankle and being unable to flee before the assassin took the staircase down to him.

Kramer thought desperately about how he might create some diversion. Looking around his apartment his eyes caught sight of the large arm chair..He tried picking it up and found he could with considerable effort. Using all his strength, he lifted it and managed to swing it with all his strength against the window. The frame broke, the glass panes shattered and the chairman fell with the debris, hitting the courtyard floor with a loud crash.

As quietly as he could, Kramer opened his apartment dour and peered outside. There was no sign of anyone hiding around the corner. The stairs leading to the basement were in the opposite direction, about twenty feet from his apartment. He decided to chance it, to race for the stairs and hope the assassin had been fooled by the diversion to go down to the courtyard. Instead of proceeding to the stairs as quietly as possible, Kramer elected to run to lessen the risk of the assassin catching up to him. In the basement he sped past the corridor leading to the courtyard and raced down the long one running the length of the building to the parking lot. His car was parked quite far from the building, but he reached it without hearing any pursuit. Kramer gunned his car and sped out of the parking lot and to the parkway leading north to Maryland. Periodically he checked his rear view mirror for signs he was being followed; happily there were none.

Pulling up in front of Amy Yoder's home, Kramer was pleased to find her car parked in the driveway. He raced up to the front door and pounded it. Amy's happy expression which greeted him quickly evaporated as he said, "Amy, you've got to get out of your house immediately. They just tried to kill me in my apartment. I'm afraid they may come here for you. If you can find the bills we found in the safety deposit box that would be helpful, but we can't spend time looking for them."

She ran into another room and returned with a triumphant grin on her face. "Here they are," she said, handing Kramer the bills. "Do you want me to get the box key? It's in the refrigerator as you suggested."

"No, it should be safe there. Let's go."

They hurried into his car and they sped off. Kramer made several turns to discourage pursuit, although he was unable to spot anyone following them. His concentration on evading possible pursuers and in reaching a safe haven was so great he was able to answer her questions only in monosyllables. After some fifteen minutes he relaxed and he drove on north to the Capital Beltway which circles Washington.

At the intersection with the Beltway he found what he had been looking for, a collection of hotels and motels situated there to serve long-distance travelers. He headed to the shabbiest looking motel and pulled up in its parking lot. "I hate to put you in a place like this, Amy," he said, "They rent rooms here by the hour. I chose it because they are less likely to be suspicious of a couple arriving in the middle of the day without luggage than in one of the nicer places."

He registered at the desk as Mr. and Mrs. Johnson, listing a Richmond, Virginia false address. As he expected, the desk clerk raised no questions, accepting without comment the hundred dollar bill he used to pay the overnight charge. Their room, as he expected, was well-worn, with an antiquated TV set and only one lamp that worked. However, he was pleased when he pulled back the bedspread to see that the sheets were clean.

When she asked him again the reason for his obvious concern, this time he answered at length. He recounted in detail his phone conversation with Cameron, Cameron's reaction which seemed to indicate awareness of the murder and the effort by an alleged plumber to enter his apartment.

Her expression when he finished showed she shared his fears. "What should we do?" she asked.

"I don't think we have any choice. We won't be safe as long as Cameron is alive. We have to kill him."

She shook her head. "We can't be sure it was Cameron. And even if it is, I can't approve of taking anyone's life. I don't think I can tell you what to do. You know so much more about these things than I do. But please don't ask me to help you."

He saw that she was determined. "Certainly, Amy," he answered softly. "I can understand. I hate to do it myself. I'll handle it. You won't be involved."

To kill Cameron, the first thing Kramer had to do was to locate his home address. He decided to try the method that had proved successful in locating Tillman's address, consulting the phone directories. He looked through the desk and table drawers in his room but could find none. He thought of asking at the desk, but doubted that would be any more successful. He would have to go to the nearest public library.

"I'm going to go to the public library," he told Amy, "Would you like to come with me?"

"Yes," she answered, "It would be nice to get out."

They went back down to the lobby and out to his car. "Do you know where the nearest library is?" he asked her.

"Sorry, no. This is not a part of the county I'm familiar with. He stopped to ask at a gas station and obtained directions. The library when he got to it was smaller than the one he had used in Washington, but they did have local phone directories. Because many of the middle and senior grade Agency employees seemed to live in Montgomery County he decided to try that phone directory first. He was pleasantly surprised to find a Robert S. Cameron listed, although he couldn't be certain it was the right Cameron.

Kramer copied down Cameron's address and then looked around the library to find Amy. He discovered her in the fiction selection. "Did you find Cameron's address?" she asked when she saw him.

"I think so. Do you want to come with me while I try to make certain?"

She agreed, adding that she wanted to check out a couple of books she had found to have something to read in the motel. He thought of telling her not to in case Cameron had someone screening events in the area to locate them, then changed his mind. If Cameron learned they were still in Montgomery County it would not materially assist hi and there was no reason to get Amy any more worried than she already was.

With the aid of his area map, Kramer was able to find the street on which Cameron's house was located. It was past even and it was possible that Cameron, if this was his home, had already arrived. He decided to wait a bit, pulling up several house away. The neighborhood was an upper income one much like the one in which Tillman had lived, although these were a bit larger and several sported swimming pools.

As Kramer and Amy watched carefully, a limo drove up and deposited a man at Cameron's home. There was no doubt. It was Cameron. He turned and told Amy. She looked at him pensively. "What do we do now?" she inquired.

"We go home. We've done enough for today." He asked if she were hungry, and when she answered he was, they stopped at a fast-food restaurant and had hamburgers and soft drinks. She declined his suggestion that they stop for ice cream, but when he did so accompanied him into the restaurant and ordered ice cream along with him.

Back in the hotel room, they relaxed watching TV. About ten, Kramer felt exhausted. "I'm ready to turn in," he said to Amy. "Why don't you take the bed and I'll sleep on the couch." He took off and hung up his outer clothing. Having no pajamas, he would by necessity sleep in his underwear. Looking for some extra blankets in the closet, he saw out of the corner of his eye Amy also stripping down to her bra and panties."

Kramer got down on the couch, struggling to find a comfortable position. "Ed," Amy said, "Why don't you sleep in here with me? I don't mind."

It was an offer he'd be stupid to refuse. He climbed into the bed, trying to make sure she had enough room. He was starting to doze off when he felt her move close, touching him. "Ed, she whispered softly, "Please put your arm around me. I'm frightened."

As s he did so, he felt body press tight against him, her body warm and tender. It had been years since he had slept with a woman. Without thinking, he kissed her softly on the neck. She turned around abruptly and kissed him passionately on the lips. In seconds they were making love.

The next morning Kramer awakened with sunlight streaming into the room through the window. Opening his eyes he saw Amy standing by the bathroom door drying her towel. "Good morning," she said," I've just taken my shower; the bathroom's all yours. He climbed out of bed and went into the bathroom to shave. He was in the midst of shaving when Amy entered the bathroom.

"Ed," she said , "I had a lot of fun last night. But I don't want you to feel that you owe me anything. We're friends."

He grabbed a face towel and whipped the shaving cream from his face. He then walked over to her, grabbed her and kissed her. " Amy," he told her. "You're more than just a good lay to me. I really like you."

They both dressed and Kramer suggested they go out for breakfast. In the lobby, he paid the clerk for a second night's stay, leaving the latter with a surprised look on his face. Apparently, very few of his guests stayed for more than a night.

Kramer found a fast food restaurant nearby. As they sat down, he suggested that they eat lightly as he thought it might be fun for them to go out to an early dinner at a more upscale restaurant than they had eaten in thus far. After they finished eating and were back in the car he drove until he found a shopping mall with a large department store. "Let's go in and buy you some clothing," he told her. "I remember how my ex-wife hated to wear the same clothes more than one day. She made a halfhearted protest, then accompanied him into the store laughing.

Amy limited her purchases to some lingerie until they passed through the women's dress section. Kramer spotted a dress he thought would look good on Amy and persuaded her to try it on. In part he wanted to do something nice for her; in part he wanted to find a pleasant way of passing time until they were ready for dinner. He was pleased when she decided to buy the dress and agreed with his suggestion that she put it on.

They drove for about an hour after leaving the department store as Kramer looked for a good restaurant. He was not familiar with Montgomery County and had no tourist literature to guide him. Eventually he spotted a steak house whose name he remembered reading about The meal was as pleasant as he had hoped it would be and he found Amy's conversation extremely interesting. He was surprise to learn that after earning an advanced degree in library science she had been a reference librarian at Georgetown University and had reluctantly given it up at the insistence of her husband, who wanted her home early.

It was late afternoon by the time they arrived back at the motel. In the room, Kramer told Amy that he would go now to Cameron's home and complete his surveillance. "Would you like me to go with you?" she asked.

"I don't think it would be much sense," he answered, trying to sound sincere. "I'll be staying late to monitor all their comings and goings. I've done it before and it's extremely boring. If you have to go to the bathroom, you use a cup. And you can't divert yourself with conversation for fear of not paying full attention to the job."

"All right," she said. "You've convinced me."

He kissed Amy, then went down to the car and drove off, feeling guilty at deceiving her. If everything went well , he planned to kill Cameron tonight. It was not something she would want to know and there was no sense in burdening her with the information.

On his way to Cameron's house, Kramer stopped at a hardware store. He bought a crowbar to use in prying open doors and windows, a glass cutter and a large hammer. The latter, would serve a double purpose; it could also be used as a bludgeon, if decided to dispatch Cameron that way.

Once again he parked several houses away from Cameron's. He watched as a boy about fourteen, probably Cameron's son, arrived home carrying school books. A bit later a woman, probably Mrs. Cameron, pulled into the driveway and walked with two younger school age children into the house. Finally, well past seven, Cameron arrived home in a chauffeur-driven car that resembled the one he had seen used by Tillman.

Time passed with agonizing slowness as Kramer sat crouched down in his car, carefully watching the house. It had been many years since he last engaged in a car surveillance and his muscles had grown less forgiving with age. Night fell and the lights came on in the lower floor of Cameron's home.

76

About nine, lights came on in the upstairs bedrooms. Some time later, the downstairs lights were turned off, followed one by one by the bedroom lights.

It was almost eleven when the last of the bedroom lights was turned off. It was now time for Kramer to act on the half-formed plan that he had in his mind. He would force open a back window with his crowbar, move upstairs, find Cameron's bedroom and kill him with the aid of the hammer. He hoped he would not have to injure Cameron's wife who presumably would be in the same bedroom. Kramer was aware it was not much of a plan, but he was desperate.

One major problem was that Cameron's wife and children might see his face and be able to describe his appearance to the police. He regretted not buying a face mask or stocking to conceal his face. As a makeshift substitute, he took the plastic bag he had used to carry the tools he had purchased at the hardware store and tore holes in it for his eyes and mouth.

Kramer was about to put his plan into operations when he saw headlights appear at the corner of the street and a taxi speed down it in his direction. It pulled up along side his car, the rear door opened and Amy got out and ran toward him. "You haven't killed him yet, have you?" she said, desperation in her voice., as the taxi sped off.

"No, I haven't killed anything?" he reassured her. "What are you doing here?"

She got into the car next to him. "Thank God," she said, as much to herself as to Kramer. "Turning to him, she added, "You can't kill him."

"Amy, I thought you agreed it had to be done to save our own lives."

"You don't understand," Amy pressed him. "Back in the motel I thought of what you had told me about your phone conversation with Cameron's secretary. You gave her your correct name and mentioned my husband's death in Vienna. If it looks like Cameron was murdered, the police will probably question her. She is likely to tell them about what you said to her and you'd be arrested."

Kramer was shocked. He had forgotten about what he told Cameron's secretary. Amy was right. There was a good chance that if he killed the Deputy Director, the police would come looking for him. He could claim as an alibi he had spent the night in the motel room with Amy, but that would also seem suspicious. The police might well conclude he had plotted with Amy to murder her husband. Cursing silently, Kramer started the car and drove back to the motel, wondering how he could have been so stupid. Only Amy's quick wits had saved him from a terrible blunder.

Although he rarely drank, Kramer wanted a stiff drink to calm his nerves. He could find no bars open; finally he stopped at an open convenience store and bought a large container of hot chocolate as a substitute. Amy laughed when he suggested buying one for her, but back in the motel room she shared his. When he finished the hot chocolate he quickly undressed and threw himself on the bed, seeking forgetfulness in sleep. He awakened the next morning, as depressed as he had been the night before.

Seeking to comfort him Amy said, "Isn't there anyone on the Agency who can help us?"

He shook his head. "There's nobody in the Agency I know I can trust."

"If Cameron was in charge of the embezzlement,"she persisted, "Then his superiors wouldn't be likely to be involved. You could go to one of them."

"the troubles is," he answered," There are only two people above Cameron, the Director and the Deputy Director."

"What about one of them?"

"I don't know what I could get to Parish, the Director. He doesn't know me. If I called and managed to get through to him, all he'd do is tell me to talk to one of my superiors. He really knows little about clandestine operations; he started off in one of the Congressional offices and then spent his career in the Federal Budget Office before the President named him CIA Director."

Kramer thought for a minute. "You know," he said slowly, "I might try the Deputy Director. Trent is an Admiral, but he's had a lot intelligence work Before he was named Deputy Director he was head of the National Security Agency."

"Do you know him?" Amy asked.

"No, but I know he lives at the Washington Navy Yard. I think I might be able to get to see him there."

The glimmer of a plan, no matter how tenuous, lifted Kramer's spirits. As he dressed, he asked Amy for her preferences in going for breakfast. It was a Saturday and she remembered reading about a nice Saturday buffets at one of the nearby hotels. After they had eaten a sumptuous meal accompanied by champagne. Kramer took the opportunity to look up the telephone number of the Washington Navy Yard. Using a hotel phone booth, he called Admiral Wright's residence. To the man who picked up the phone, he gave his name and added that he was a case officer on the Russian Desk and urgently needed to speak to the Admiral.

A minute passed and he heard a crisp voice say "This is Admiral Wright."

"Sir, Kramer said," I apologize for calling you at home but its urgent that I meet with you today. May I come over now?"

"Mr. Kramer," the Admiral answered. "Today is Saturday and I have just come home from the Agency. I have a golf game scheduled for this afternoon. If you wish to see me, I suggest you call my office on Monday t o schedule an appointment."

This was the response Kramer was dreading. He had to persuade Admiral Wright to see him. As earnestly s he could he said. "Admiral, I know this is Saturday. This is literally a matter of life and death. During my work on the Russian Desk I discovered a massive embezzlement of unvouchered Agency funds. High-level officials are involved. I don't know anyone at the Agency I can trust to talk to below your level."

There was a minute of silence before Kramer heard the Admiral say, "All right, come over. I'll give orders to the security at the gate to admit you."

Kramer hung up the phone and rejoined Amy, who was waiting for him in the hotel lobby. When he recounted his conversation with the Admiral she brightened up. "Thank God," she said, "It sounds like he'll help."

"I'm not sure of that," he answered. "But at least it's a foot in the door."

Amy offered to drive with him to the Admiral's residence. However, he dropped her off at the motel with the excuse it might complicate things if Wright saw them together. In truth, he wanted to be along as he drove to plan out his comments to the Admiral. At the Washington Navy Yard Kramer gave his name to the guards at the gate, was given instructions to aid him in finding Admiral Wright's quarters and was passed in.

The Admiral's residence was at the end of a circular drive, a large building dating back to the early twentieth century. Kramer parked in front of the house, walked up to the door and knocked. The door was opened by a man wearing what looked like a navy mess stewards jacket. His crew cut and sharp eyes led Kramer to believe the man was either navy or CIA security.

Kramer was led into a study and found Agency Deputy Director seated behind a desk. He studied the Admiral as he never had seen Wright before. The Admiral looked in his mid fifties, with an erect stature which had the effect of making him look taller than his five and a half feet height. The expression on Wright's face as he stared at Kramer was anything but cordial.

"Mr. Kramer," he said in a cold voice. You lied to me. I took the trouble to check you out with personnel. Your are not with the Russian Desk. You resigned from the Agency several months ago."

"Yes, sir," Kramer answered, trying to sound more confident than he felt. "I did resign from the Agency several months ago. But I did not lie to you, although I did give you the impression I was still with CIA. I was afraid that otherwise you would not agree to see me. I told you I learned about the embezzlement while I was on the Russian Desk, which is true. I also told you it was a matter of life and death, which is also true."

"You're splitting hairs."

" Please, sir, Kramer implored, just hear me out."

"All right," the Admiral, agreed, "I'll give you five minutes. What's this about the embezzlement?"

Kramer began with his letter to the Deputy Director of Operations requesting retirement, his being summoned to Tillman's office, and Brewster's statements to him about his resignation being approved but his retirement denied. "Mr. Kramer," the Admiral interrupted, "There is no individual in that office named Brewster. "

"I found that out later, sir."

Before Admiral Wright could order him to leave, Kramer hurried to repeat Brewster's comments about the high-level-defector named Howard and the offer of his pension if he liquidated Howard for the Agency."

The Admiral's face clouded over. He once again interrupted Kramer's narrative, saying in a cold voice, "There has been no high-level defector. I think you had better leave."

"Sir," Kramer said, "I killed Howard in Vienna using the lethal injection kit Brewster gave me. Later on I found out that the Howard's real name was Thomas Yoder and that he worked in the Agency's Finance Division."

"You actually killed Howard?"

"Yes, sir," Kramer answered.

The Admiral picked up the phone he had on his desk, saying, "I think this is a matter for the police."

"That would be foolish."

Wright stared at Kramer with amazement, clearly unused to being spoken to in such fashion. "In the first place," Kramer said, "When the police got here, I'd deny I said anything about killing Yoder. There's no proof. Brewster told me the injection was undetectable and Yoder's body was cremated. Even more important for the Agency, if you don't investigate, you continue to have a senior CIA official continuing his embezzlement of a large amount of money. Everything I've told you, strange as it is, is the truth. Would anyone be crazy enough to make up a story like that?"

The Admiral put back the phone. "No, I give you that."

Taking the opportunity, Kramer quickly recited his contact with Tillman and the latter's sudden death before he could communicate his findings to Kramer, his identification of Howard as Yoder with the aid of Mrs. Yoder and the attempt to kill him in his apartment."

When he had finished, Wright said, "That's an interesting story. Do you have any proof?"

"Yes, sir." Taking Yoder's passport out of his jacket pocket and handing it to the Admiral, Kramer said, "This was in Yoder's safety deposit box. In the rear, you will find a stamp showing Yoder traveled to Zurich some two months before I killed him in Vienna. There is also a slip of paper I found in the passport with the name of a Zurich bank and a number which looks like the number of a Swiss bank account.

"That's scarcely proof."

"Mrs. Yoder told me her husband had made only two trips out of the country. The first was this one t o Zurich. The second was the one to Vienna where I killed him. He was registered at the Vienna hotel under the name of Howard, showing he traveled there using a false passport."

"Isn't it possible that he was on an official mission for the Agency?"

"If it was an official mission, why would Brewster want me to kill him?"

Wright thought for a minute. "So what you're saying is that Yoder embezzled the money from the Agency, put it into a numbered Swiss account under his own name and that someone in the Agency had you kill him to obtain the money?"

"Yes, sir."

"Who is this mysterious someone and how is he connected to Brewster?"

"I don't know who Brewster is," Kramer admitted, "But the one in charge is Robert Cameron, the Deputy Director for Operations. I confirmed he was by telling him I knew about the death of Thomas Yoder in Vienna and the death of Mr. Tillman. His reaction was of someone trying to cover it up. Then someone tried to kill me in my apartment the next day."

"I assume, the Admiral said, "That your goal in telling me this is to have me investigate the embezzlement and to establish Cameron is involved."

"Yes, sir. As long as Cameron has a senior position in the Agency, he will try to use it to have me killed. And I also want to get the pension I earned."

"Fair enough," Wright replied. Taking Yoder's passport and the slip of paper with the number. "I'll look into your story."

Kramer realized that the Admiral had still not accepted his story as valid. "One last thing,sir," he added. Mr. Tillman was quite interested in the passport Brewster had prepared for me to use in traveling to Vienna. You might look into that."

On his way back to the motel, Kramer reviewed in his mind what he had told Wright. He had not been as successful as he might have wished. All he could do now was wait and hope.

Two months later, Mr. and Mrs. Edward Kramer stood at the first-class section of the United Airlines counter in Dulles Airport. They were there to pick up their tickets for that day's flight to London, where they would spend their honeymoon. Amy Kramer's left hand sported a large diamond ring which she had inherited from her mother and which Kramer re-sized as a wedding gift for his bride.

On the previous day, Kramer had attended a retirement ceremony in his honor at the Agency at which he had been presented with the highest medal awarded by CIA. The Agency Deputy Director Admiral Wright told the assembled guests that the medal had been awarded Kramer in recognition of his outstanding performance and exceptional dedication to duty in the face of hazardous conditions.

As Kramer bid the Admiral goodbye and expressed his thanks for the latter's kind comments,l Wright informed Kramer that his first retirement check would be deposited in his bank account in two weeks. He also told Kramer that an extensive investigation had uncovered a large-scale embezzlement of Agency funds. No evidence had been found that Deputy Director f or Operations Robert Cameron was involved. However, Cameron had submitted his resignation from CIA upon being informed that if he did not do so, a letter of censure would be placed in his file rebuking him for the unauthorized issuance of an American passport in violation of Agency regulations and procedures.

The Kramer's picked up their tickets, went through security and several hours later boarded the flight to London. As the plane took off Amy, who disliked flying, grabbed Kramer's arm and held on tightly. "Dear," she said, trying to divert her mind from thinking about flying, "do you have any idea as to who Brewster is?"

He laughed. "Amy," he answered quietly, "Some things, you never know.

THE SAUDI PLOT

As befitted his position as President, George Baker sat at the head of the table, looking at his Cabinet members. He was a tall man, well over six feet, and his lean, muscular frame accentuated the appearance of height. Critics of his administration asserted that he owed his successful career in the army, he had risen to be a full general and Army Chief of Staff, to his height rather than to his skill as a military man. The more astute knew that his nomination as President was due to the fear in his party that they would be unable to win the presidency unless they chose a popular military hero as their nominee.

On Baker's right sat Richard Hunter, the National Security Adviser. Unlike previous occupants of the position, Hunter had had no previous experience in international affairs; an elections analyst, he had gotten close to the President as a result of directing Baker's successful campaign for the nomination and then the presidency. Possibly because of his background, Hunter construed national security affairs to be limited to what affected the president's political position and the advancement of his personal agenda.

Baker stared at his watch and then opened the meeting; it was not his custom to wait for the arrival of late-comers. "All right," he said, "Let's begin the meeting. It should be a short one; there are only two items on the agenda, a proposed trans-pacific trade agreement and the level of agricultural subsidies." Turning to Secretary of State Rogers, sitting directly next to him on his left, he said, "Mr. Rogers, please summarize the pros and cons of the proposed trans-pacific trade agreement."

The Secretary's comments were interrupted as the door opened and CIA Director James Collins entered and then stopped, realizing that the meeting had begun without him. His face reddened, and he said in a low voice, "I apologize for being late; I had to take an emergency call from the Operations Center." Rather than taking his seat at the foot of the table, Collins walked up to the President and began whispering to him.

Baker's face clouded over. "Damn it!" he exclaimed, "Has this been confirmed? "Yes, sir. It's from a source of unimpeachable accuracy." "This is important; tell everyone about it!" Complying with the President's order, Collins said, in a grave voice, " The King of Saudi Arabia has called in our ambassador and informed him that his country is seizing full control of all oil properties in the county. All Western companies and Western technicians are to be expelled and to the extent their expertise is vital, it is to be supplied by Russian technicians. Saudi Arabia will more than double the price for its oil to two hundred dollars per barrel and cut its exports to the level required to keep the world price that high. All this will be done within the next two weeks. " "That's ridiculous," the Secretary of State burst out. "We would have had some inkling of this being planned." "It's completely correct in every way," Collins answered. "The King told this directly to the Ambassador and the Embassy sent this in. I was informed by the Agency Operations Center. You will receive the same report in a minute or two from the Department; I got it first because our communications system is just a bit quicker." The National Security Adviser shook his head. "This is serious," he said to the President. "I wish we weren't so close to the next elections." The concern he felt obvious on his face, Rogers said, "If Saudi Arabia goes through with this plans, it will mean financial chaos around the world. The countries that rely on imported petroleum like Japan and France will have to drastically raise taxes, impose oil rationing and cut other imports. Their currencies will plummet. The United States can probably get by with increased oil from our domestic shale oil producers, but our exporters will face sharp reductions in the amount of goods sold abroad." There was general agreement around the table from the other participants. "All right, the President," said " What's our response? What do you recommend?" The Secretary of Energy, the first Muslim every appointed to the Cabinet, volunteered, " I think I have a good relationship with the King. Why don't I go there on a special mission and ask him to reconsider?".

Collins shook his head. "That's equivalent to doing nothing. Unless we do something immediately, the genie is out of the bottle. "

President Barker nodded in agreement. "The obvious solution is to remove the king." "Remove him? Specifically, what do you mean by that?" the CIA Director asked.

"Damn it!" Barker exploded again. He clearly did not take kindly to hearing any response to one of his orders but "yes sir."

"Liquidate him! I don't care how. I don't want to hear the details. Just do it! " Hooked, Collins stared in disbelief. Didn't Baker realize the impossibility of carrying out his order? He started to say something, then stopped. The President, he knew, would not listen to him. He looked about the room, praying that one of the others closer to the President would object. No one did. He looked to the Vice President, the widely-respected former governor of New York. The Vice President shrugged and averted his gaze.

"All right," the President said. "The first item on our agenda today is the trade agreement."

Collins remained silent throughout the meeting. He did not linger behind when it was over, as he did on most such occasions. Instead, he left the room without speaking further to any of the other participants and headed directly to where his car was parked, instructing the driver to take him back to the Agency. As they headed south along the beautiful Potomac River he went over the Cabinet meeting in his mind, wondering if he should have said something else, what his options were, what he should do. By the time they had reached the Agency, parked the car and he had taken his personal elevator to the to his office on the top floor, he had made up his mind. Entering his office, he instructed his secretary to cancel all of his appointments and summon the Deputy Director of Operations and the Chief of Middle East and South Asian Division to come immediately.

Because his office was just down the corridor, the first to arrive was Ross Chapman. Chapman held a key post, Deputy Director for Operations. In that capacity, he directly ran the Agency's espionage operations and direct covert actions. Chapman and Collins, both had served the bulk of their careers in the CIA Far East Division and knew each other well. Collins' previous post before his designation as CIA Director had been as Chief of the Far East Division, with Chapman serving as his head of the Japan Branch. Chapman and Collins chatted amiably for a few minutes until Joe Featherstone, Chief of the-the Middle East and South Asian Division arrived from his office two floors below.

Featherstone was one of the Agency's few good Arabic language officers. He had been promoted rapidly through the ranks, his career having been boosted by his recruitment of a key member of an Islamic terrorist group. The recruitment, in fact, had produced no useful results, the agent having been assassinated by a rival group before he could provide any important information.

Before getting down to the reason for the meeting, Collins offered each of them a cup of coffee, which they eagerly accepted. Coffee in the Director's office was always a treat; the beverage served made from the finest Ethiopian coffee beans. The coffee beans had been presented to Collins personally as a present by the Director of the Ethiopian intelligence service.

Because the value of the gift was estimated as well over a hundred dollars, Collins had been constrained by agency regulations fro accepting the gift until a helpful member of the Legal Council's office had suggested the subterfuge of accepting it as a gift to the agency.

The CIA Director allowed his subordinates to enjoy their coffee before broaching the distasteful discussion he was going to have with them. When the coffee was finished, Chapman and Featherstone turned toward Collins.

"Gentlemen," he said, "We have a problem. A big problem." He proceeded to give them a detailed account of what had transpired at the Cabinet meeting.

Featherstone was the first to respond. "You said he order the 'liquidation' of the King . Just what does he mean by that?"

Collins shrugged. "He didn't specify. They way he said it, I'm sure he meant he wanted the King dead. When I tried to get him to explain he ordered me to carry out his orders and not to bother him with the details."

"Doesn't he realize that's illegal?" Chapman asked. "We would go to jail for that. And if we killed the King and it became known abroad, we'd be tried for a war crime by an international tribunal."

Featherstone nodded his head in agreement. "Didn't you try to explain that to the President? What about Secretary Rogers and Hunter? Didn't they tell him it couldn't be done? "

"I don't think he knows or cares about what's illegal," Collins said. "He's aware that things like that were done during the Vietnam War and sees no reason we can't do that now. Nobody at the Cabinet meeting said anything to dissuade him, not Rogers or Hunter, not even the Vice President. My only choice was to resign. I considered doing that, but it would have been of no use. He made it pretty clear he'd keep on firing officials until he found someone to carry out his order. At least by staying in place, I may be able to protect the Agency for other stupid actions."

"Suppose all three of us threaten to resign?" Chapman asked. "Maybe then he would back down."

"I don't think that would do any good," Collins answered. "Beyond that, it's not a completely foolish idea. If the King carries out his plans concerning oil, it will cause an economic and financial catastrophe for much of the world."

"So what do we do?" Chapman asked.

"Gentlemen," Collins said. "I think I will follow the lead of the President. I am transmitting the President's order to you and giving you the responsibility for carrying it out. I don't want to know the details. Just do it."

Featherstone and Chapman stared at each other wondering if Collins was joking. After a minute of silence, they realized he wasn't. "Just do it," he repeated.

His two subordinates stood up. Only Chapman said goodbye as they left the Director's and walked down the corridor t o Chapman's office. They sat down, and Featherstone asked, "Any idea, other than resigning?"

"I guess we have no choice but to do it," the Deputy Director said. "The question really is how."

Featherstone thought for a minute. "You know, I think we ought to bring in the Saudi desk chied Tom Stewart. It clearly would fall within his area of responsibility, and he knows all the actors in Saudi Arabia. He's also a first-class officer."

"That's an excellent idea," Chapman said. "And I also think we ought to get Bob Golden. He's the lawyer the General Counsels' Office assigned to provide close support to the Operations Directorate. He's good and is used to telling us ways of doing what is necessary while technically remaining within the law." Chapman picked up his phone and instructed his secretary to send for Stewart and Golden.

When Stewart and Golden arrived, Chapman repeated to them that the President had told Collins, quoting President Barker's exact language regarding the liquidation of the Saudi King.

"You don't have to tell me it's illegal," he told Golden. "What we need is some way of carrying out that order and not being accused of doing something illegal."

Golden stared at them. "That's a tough one," he said. "How to make something illegal legal. They didn't go into that at Harvard Law School." The others sat quietly as the young lawyer mulled over the problem.

"You know," he said after a few minutes of reflection, "There is no way in the world to assassinate the King legally. There's not anything, not even a Presidential finding, that would justify such an action. However, there may be a way. If

95

the Agency undertook some action that was legal and the King was unfortunately killed in collateral damage, that would not appear to me to be illegal."

Chapman and Featherstone exchanged grins. "Bob," Chapman said, "I think you may have something there. Probably it would be best if you left now. We don't want you to lose your virginity."

Golden rose with and smiled. "I've already forgotten everything that was said here," he said, leaving the room.

"All right," Chapman told the others. "Bob's given us an answer to our problem if we are smart enough to figure out how to use it. Tom," he added. "I am assigning you full responsibility for handling this operation. Joe can assign someone to fill in for you as Saudi desk officer."

Stewart nodded his acceptance. "What code name do we give to this operation?" "None," Chapman answered. "I don't want to make it easy for someone later to retrieve the correspondence about this operation from our computers and put the pieces together. You will report only to Joe or me on this operation a and slug it for our eyes only. We'll know what you are working on without your having to go into detail." "I understand."

"Good," the Deputy Director said. "Now Tom, do you have any thoughts about how to proceed? Remember, the liquidation has to be accomplished within two weeks."

"To begin with, we don't have time to mount a coup against the King. We don't even have any assets to head such a coup. We can't assassinate him in a shooting or bombing.

There is too much chance of our agent being caught and the CIA's role exposed."

"You know," Featherstone interrupted, "It might be desirable to leave them uncertain about our involvement. If we simply kill the King, it's quite possible the next member of the Royal Family in line would pursue the same policy. Our primary objective is to get them to abandon the oil nationalization scheme and keep Western technicians operating their oil fields."

"Suppose," Stewart speculated. "The Saudi's arrest some American citizens and hold them as hostages. We'd have a good justification for going in there militarily to rescue the hostages and see that the King is killed in the fighting. "

"That's a great idea," Featherstone said, "But how do we ensure that the Saudi's take American hostages? I very much doubt they'd be stupid enough to do that."

Stewart laughed. "Let me take care of that," he said. " I have some good contacts in the Saudi Security Service in Riyadh. I am pretty sure can persuade them to put some Americans in jail. With a little luck, they will be confined in a prison near the Royal Palace. We arrange an air rescue operation which necessitates neutralizing the Saudi anti-aircraft missile defenses in the vicinity of the jail. It would, of course, be a regrettable mistake when the attack on the anti-aircraft emplacements inadvertently hit the Palace."

Chapman shook his head doubtfully. "I don't think we can order the Air Force to attack the Palace. It would leave a record."

Stewart laughed again. "Naturally, we wouldn't tell the Air Force to bomb the Palace. We would carefully give them the coordinates of the Saudi missiles to prevent such a mistake. Unfortunately, through a clerical error, the coordinates provided would be those of the Palace."

"Can you pull it off?" Featherstone asked.

"I can. I think it would be better if I did not go into the details. I'll arrange things and then send you word to order the rescue operations. You can start the arrangements for that now."

Chapman looked at Featherstone. It sounds good to me. "What's your opinion?" "I concur," he answered. "It's the only real alternative we have." The Director of Operations turned back to Stewart. "Start work on it immediately. If necessary, you can give orders in my name to anyone in the Directorate. Draw any funds you require. Allot all expenditures to other projects. We don't want a record that this operation every existed. I'll provide any paperwork or authorizations you need. If anyone gives you trouble tell them to get in touch with me." "Yes, sir." Stewart stood. "I'll start now. He left the office. As the door closed behind him, Chapman turned to Featherstone. "Honestly Joe, do you think he can pull it off? " "Sure," the Division Chief answered smiling wryly. "When elephants can fly." He left Chapman alone. The latter rose and walked over to the window, where stood and looked out at the beautiful Virginia countryside. "God help us all now," he said to himself.

When Stewart got down to the Saudi Desk, he sat for a while quietly, planning the operation. When he had completed the plan in his mind, he drew up a travel order authorizing him to travel to Riyadh for an inspection trip to the Riyadh Station. He had been there less than four months early on such a trip, but no one would question a Desk Chief visiting his Station if he thought it necessary.

To save time, Stewart carried his travel authorization himself back to Featherstone's office. When he gave Featherstone his request, the latter signed it immediately. "Going off to inspect Riyadh," he said, winking as he did so. "Have a successful trip."

Returning to his office, Stewart unlocked his safe and removed his personal cash box. He removed the several thousand dollars in cash he kept there for operational expenses. That, he thought, should be more than enough to cover his trip and any additional expenses. If he required more, he could always draw it from the Riyadh Station, although it would preferable for them to know as little about his trip as possible. Replacing the cash with a scribbled, signed note, stating the amount had been taken for another project, the Desk Chief .

Stewart returned the cash box to the safe and from another drawer retrieved his diplomatic passport. He had another regular passport in the same drawer which was in a cover identity and which he sometimes used on operational trips. He had considered using it, but decided instead on the diplomatic passport, although it might compromise the security of his mission.

If the operation ended in failure, however, the diplomatic passport provided Stewart with a good measure of protection. The State Department and the CIA could not refrain from taking strong action to free him from a Saudi prison as they might well prefer to do to avoid unfavorable publicity. Stewart believed he was as patriotic as any other American, but he had no intention of spending the next dozen years in a Saudi jail.

Following the usual procedure in arranging for travel, the Desk Officer called the agency travel section and instructed them to obtain tickets for him to travel from Washington to Riyadh on the following day. The date for his return trip was to be left open as he had no firm idea of when he would be able to finish his mission in Saudi Arabia.

The Travel Section called back to tell him that he was booked on the six pm. direct Saudi Airlines flight from Dulles to Riyadh, but that because of the time required to process his request, it would not be possible to put him on the next day's flight. It was only after Stewart cited the emergency nature of his trip and invoked the Director's name that the travel clerk agree to put him on the next day's flight and to have the tickets personally delivered to his home before noon tomorrow.

Stewart left the Headquarters Building as soon as the arrangements were completed to return home. He needed to pack and to break the news to his wife, Mary, that he would be going away so soon after returning from his last trip.

The desk chief and his family lived in a Virginia suburb only a few minutes drive from the Agency. The Stewart's had opted for that location, although they could have bought a more modern, larger home further out, because of his belief, subsequently confirmed, that as a Desk Chief he would be obliged to work late and might be summoned back to the office at any hour to handle emergencies.

Arriving home, Stewart found his wife Mary correcting test papers. Since returning from their last tour in Saudi Arabia, she had been teaching economics at the local high school. He walked over to her and kissed her neck, causing her to laugh. "Hi, dear," he said, "I'm home."

"So I see. I'm glad you identified yourself. I might have thought it was the iceman." Her sense of humor was one of the things he liked most about her. He had met her at the Agency some twelve years earlier, when she was assigned to the Egyptian Desk as a Reports Officer and he was on the desk, handling agents in the Egyptian branch of the Muslim Brotherhood. He had been attracted first by her good looks and only later appreciated her keen intelligence. It had taken only a few dates for him to decide he would like to marry her, but it had taken almost a year for her to accept his proposal" Stewart was about to suggest Mary accompany him upstairs to the bedroom, when he heard a cry of glee and his four-year old daughter Dot ran into the room. "Daddy," she cried, "Look at what I did at school." She proudly showed him a large sheet of paper on which she had succeeded to writing her name.

"That's great, Dot," he said picking her up and hugging her. Although she was only in a pre-school day care center, the teacher there had started teaching a few of the brighter children to write their names. Stewart was very grateful his daughter had inherited not only his wife's good looks but also her brains.

He put her back down on the floor and asked "Can you write your last name? It's spelled S-T-E-W-A-R-T."

"Let me try, Daddy," she answered and scampered off to her bedroom to find her pencil.

"Is Bobby home from school yet?" Stewart asked, referring to their ten-year old son.

Bobby was in the fifth grade of the local elementary school, only a block away from their house. The houses' proximity to the local elementary and junior high schools was one of the reasons they had purchased it.

"Yes," Mary answered. "He's playing baseball over at the school playground. He asked if he could play until dinner time and do his homework after supper. He's been working hard at school and I thought he deserved some fun."

"Sure," Stewart agreed.

"You're home early," Mary said, as she finished grading her papers. "Was it a light day."

"Far from it. I was busy at meetings virtually the entire day. I even spent a couple of hours with the Director."

"I'm impressed. Can you tell me anything about it?" "A problem came up in Riyadh," he answered. "That's why I'm home early. They want me to go to go back to Riyadh tomorrow to fix the problem." "But you were there less than a month ago." "I know," he said. I hate like Hell to go. But I have no choice." "Will you be back by Saturday?" Mary asked. "Bobby has that soccer playoff game. He was hoping you could be there and help root for his team." "No, damn it. I'll try, but most likely it will take me a week to fix the problem, possibly as much as two." "It sounds serious," she said, concern in her voice.

"It's just routine." he told her, lying to alleviate her worry. "Only a personnel problem. If I can't return within a week , I'll call you."

When Bobby returned home for dinner, he face revealed his disappointment as his father told him he would have to miss the Saturday soccer game. Both Bobby and Mary were uncharacteristically silent during diner, with only Dot laughing at Stewart's efforts to be jovial. After dinner, Stewart and his wife put Dot to bed and Bobby went off to do his homework.

As Stewart stood in the kitchen helping Mary with the dishes he said, "I have an idea. Why don't we all go off to the beach when I get home. School will be out by then."

Mary looked dubious. The water will probably still be too cool to go swimming. Why don't we hold off until later in the summer?"

"We need a break," Stewart answered. "And they'll owe me a vacation for going off to Riyadh. Later in the summer, I may not be able to get away. Anyhow," he added, "It's always fun walking along the beach and building castles in the sand with the kids."

His wife laughed. "All right," she said. "When you put it that way, how can I refuse?" The Stewart family had breakfast together the next morning. Mary offered to get home early to drive her husband to the airport, but he declined. "No need for you to have to go all the way to Dulles and back," he told her, "I'll have a taxi take me and charge it to the government." She wished him goodbye and drove off to work, taking Dot with her to drop at the nearby day care center. Bob walked his son to the elementary school. To cheer him up and make it up to Bobby for not attending the soccer match, Stewart told him about the upcoming beach vacation and promised to go fishing with his son at the beach.

Returning home, Stewart packed. His concern about the airline tickets vanished when shortly before noon a messenger from the Travel Section brought them to his house. After a light lunch, the cab he had called arrived at his home and took him to Dulles Airport. It was a bit early, but he wanted to allow enough time to go through airport security.

When he boarded the Saudi Airlines plane. Stewart was pleased to find it was not crowded. He was able to stretch out, lowering the arm rest between his seat and the seat next to him. The evening meal, served as they crossed the Atlantic, was good and he dozed off after watching a movie.

The landing in Riyadh was smooth. Stewart picked up his suitcase from the carousel and walked through the arrival lounge. He noticed that security had been beefed up since his prior visit, whether because of the planned Saudi move against Western involvement in the oil sector or because of the threat from Islamic terrorists he was not sure.

Stewart had a taxi take him to the Ritz-Carlton Hotel, which was close to the Diplomatic Quarter housing the American Embassy. Although he had not made reservations, there was no difficulty and he registered and was escorted up to his room. The room was as lovely as he had expected it to be. However, he did not have the luxury of relaxing in it for a few hours. Time was pressing.

Stewart left the hotel and walked to the American Embassy. He showed his diplomatic passport to the Marine guard on duty in the lobby and climbed the stairs to the floor housing the CIA Station. The station was familiar to him from the two previous tours he had served in Riyadh. He said hello to the secretary and without stopping walked straight into the office of Jack Barnes, the Station Chief.

Barnes looked up in surprise as someone entered his office. "Good God, Tom," he said, as soon as you recognized Stewart, "What are you doing here? I had no word you were coming." Barnes' face registered alarm. If a Desk Officer made an unscheduled visit to a Station, he often was a messenger of doom sent to convey unpleasant tidings."

"A problem came up," Stewart answered. "We had no time to alert you to my coming." "A problem?" Barnes' voice faltered.

"I' sorry, I can't. It's being kept hush-hush. But don't worry. It's got nothing to do with the Station. "

This was only partly true, but Stewart felt he had no choice but to adhere to the Director's instruction that he tell no one the reason for his trip to Riyadh. "I'll only be here a few days," Stewart added. "All I need is a room at the Station I can use and a copy of the Embassy telephone directory. I assume it lists the names of all of the Embassy staff."

"It does," Barnes assured him. He called out to his secretary to bring in a copy of the phone directory which he handed to Stewart, saying "Can't you tell me anything at all about what's going on?"

Stewart thought for a minute. Barnes was several grades senior to him. There was no sense in irritating him. Some day Stewart find himself working for Barnes. "It's a personnel matter," he Stewart explain. "They asked me to handle it because of some of the contacts I made when I was stationed here."

His answer seemed to reassure Barnes and Stewart went into the office that had been assigned him and studied all the names in the telephone directory. He returned to Barnes' office and asked "Did any of the Embassy or Station personnel return recently from being out of country?"

Barnes answered in the negative; there had been no recent returnees. Disappointed, Stewart went back to his office. With his preferred plan ruled out, Stewart turned to his plan B. He copied from the directory six names, only two of which he really was interested in; the other four names were intended only to disguise the real objects of his attention.

He then asked the Station secretary to bring him the personnel folders of all six. Protocol would have required he make the request directly to Barnes, but Stewart preferred to keep the Station Chief ignorant of as many details of his activity as possible. She came back in a minute with only three, explaining that the other three were State Department employees and not part of the Station complement. If he required the files of the State employees he would have to request them from the Embassy Personnel Officer.

Stewart had been well aware of that fact. He knew all of the officers at the Station but had been uncertain whether the two code clerk/communicators whose files he had requested belonged to the Station or to the State Department.

George Carr, the communicator he was most interested , turned out as Stewart had hoped to be a CIA employee. The file revealed Carr to be everything that Stewart had desired. He was twenty-six, young enough to be able to withstand the harsh treatment he was likely to receive in a Saudi prison. Better yet, he was unmarried. Stewart had no desire to have on his conscience creating a widow and orphans if his plan miscarried; it was bad enough to have to worry about Carr.

Stewart returned the files to the secretary, thanking her. He would have liked to ask her not to tell Barnes about his interest in them, but realized she probably would not agree. Going to the code room, he rang the bell and waited for someone to open the closed door.

"Is George Carr on duty?" he asked the code clerk who responded." "Yes, just a minute."

A minute later a young, good-looking man came to the door, a quizzical expression on his face. "I'm George Carr. Can I help you?"

"Hi" Stewart answered. "I'm Tom Stewart, the Saudi Desk Officer. In Washington they asked me to find out from you what you'd like your next foreign pot to be. There's no guarantee you'll get it, but they do try."

Carr smiled. "Gosh," he said, "I never heard they let you pick a post." "It's a new program they're experimenting with." Stewart hated having to lie to this likable young man, but he could come up with no better excuse for planting on him what was to appear incriminating evidence. He took a folded sheet of paper out of his jacket pocket and handed it to Carr.

On the sheet were three columns. The first column consisted of eight capital cities in various parts of the word. The second column consisted of eight matching last names. The third column was of various months of the year in no particular order.

Stewart explained that the cities referred to CIA Stations which would have a vacancy for a code clerk over the next twelve months. The second column indicated the name of the code clerk currently filling the position and the third the exact date his tour would be over. Stewart instructed Carr to study the forthcoming vacancies and to send him cable indicating which posts were his first, second and third choices.

"Be carefully with this sheet," Stewart told him. "It's not classified, but it could be harmful if its misplaced and some finds it. I suggest you put this sheet in your wallet for safekeeping." He was pleased to see Carr immediately following his suggestion.

Stewart said goodbye to Carr and left the Embassy. He felt badly that he was not stopping off to tell Barnes he was leaving, but it was the safer course. The less he saw of Barnes the less likely the Station Chief was to discover the details of Stewart's mission.

Back at the Ritz-Carlton Hotel he went up to his room and, picking up the room phone, dialed the number of the Saudi Interior Ministry Division of Internal Security. In his last assignment to Riyadh, Stewart had been responsible for liaison with Directorate of Investigations, that part of the ministry dealing with suppressing internal dissent. His knowledge of the Directorate and of its personnel had been the basis for his plan to carry out the President's orders to liquidate the King.

"Could I speak with Colonel Suleiman Al-Saud, please," he said when the phone was picked up. The Colonel came to the phone in a few minutes. "Colonel," Stewart began, "This is Tom Stewart. How are you?"

Stewart was pleased that the Colonel remembered him, although his tone was not as friendly as it had been in the past. "I'd like to meet with you, Colonel," he began, "Something important."

"Are you assigned back here?" Al-Saud asked.

"No, I'm here for only a few days. That's why I have to see you without delay." There was a minute of embarrassed silence. "You are aware that relations between our two governments are not as close as they used to be," the Colonel said slowly.

"What I have to tell you," Stewart went on, "Is vital. It will help you and your government. I give you my word that once you hear it, both you and the Royal Government will be very glad that you agreed to meet me."

There was a minute or two of silence as Al-Saud weighed his answer. "All right," he said. "I've just come back from lunch. Why don't I meet you about six, after work."

Looking at his watch, Stewart realized his time-table depended on meeting the Colonel immediately. "That won't work," he said, "I have to see you immediately."

Finally, the Colonel agreed to meet with Stewart in a half-hour. The site he suggested was one Stewart recognized as a small restaurant a few blocks away from the Interior Ministry and one frequented primarily by Europeans. The Colonel, Stewart decided, was reluctant to be seen meeting with Stewart by someone who might mention it to his superiors.

Stewart arrived at the restaurant at the appointed time and was shown in a table in the nearly-deserted dining-room. Al-Said arrived a few minutes later. Stewart was surprised to find him wearing a long Saudi robe, his head in a turban. Obviously, he was attempting to disguise his appearance.

The Colonel was a tall man, well-built and in his mid forties. Stewart had heard rumors that he was distantly related to the Royal family, which seemed likely considering the key post he held, Chief of Operations in the Directorate of Investigations. Ignoring any civilities, the Colonel came quickly to the point. "Why did you request this meeting. I took a considerable risk in coming here today."

"Thanks for coming," Stewart said, his sincerity apparent in his voice. "We've got a horrible mess. We've found out that one of the Station officers has been recruited by the ISIS fanatics."

"Why tell me about it?"

"Because he's involved in a plot to assassinate the King. We need your help to obtain the details."

The Colonel's face registered shock at Stewart's words. "Why don't you just arrest him and send him back to the U.S. in chains. That would eliminate the risk to the King."

"It's not that easy. First of all, if we arrest him there would be a scandal that a CIA officer is involved in plotting to assassinate your King. More importantly, Carr would just clam up. We need to know all the details; who else is involved in the plot. And when we got Carr home, we can't just hold him in jail. American law demands he be tried. We can't afford to reveal the evidence against him in an open court. It would reveal our sources and methods."

"So what do you want me to do?" Al-Saud asked.

We'd like you to arrest Carr. Put him in one of your high security Ulaysha prison and interrogate him. You can use methods we're unable to in CIA."

The Colonel smiled grimly. "We do know how to interrogate people like Carr effectively." Stewart shook his head. "Nothing too harsh. We want him kept alive. That is essential. And nothing that will permanently disable him; no pulling out his finger nails. What we suggest is strip him naked and leave him in a cold dark cell for a couple of days. Give him only a small amount of gruel to eat and awaken him at irregular times to disorient him. When you then turn him over to us it will be easy for us to extract his information and hopefully to convince him its in his interests to cooperate with us against ISIS." "You Americans are too soft," Al-Saud said contemptuously. "OK, we'll play it your way, although I can get the details of the plot a lot quicker using our standard interrogation techniques." "One thing more," Stewart added. "We believe he has in his possession a sheet of paper with the names of the other plotters and their locations. When you arrest him, search him carefully. The paper may be in his pockets or wallet. I haven't sen the sheet but one of our sources described it. Try to get Carr to explain all the notations." Stewart was pleased with himself for concocting the document and getting Carr to put it in his wallet. When the Colonel found it it would convince him of the communicator's involvement in the purported plot.

"Al-Saud stood up. "I'll get right on to it. Do you have Carr's address. We'll pick him up tonight."

"That won't work!" Stewart almost shouted. "He lives in a government apartment. We have to keep his arrest secret. You must arrest him As he leaves the Embassy this afternoon. Find some pretext to get him to get into a car with you voluntarily, then take him off to your site for interrogation."

"How will I recognize Carr? Do you have a photo of him?" Stewart shook his head. "No, I didn't have time to get one. But Carr shouldn't be hard to spot. He's twenty-six, blond-haired, blue eyes and about your height. He'll probably be wearing a bright, Hawaiian-style shirt open at the collar and tan slacks." "That should be sufficient identification," the Colonel said. "How do I get in touch with you when he's arrested?" "I'm going right back to room at the Ritz-Carlton and wait there to hear from you. Call me there as soon as you have Carr safely in the Ulaysha prison." "You'll come there?" Al-Saud asked" to help in his interrogation?" "No, I can't. As soon as I hear from you I have to get on a plane and fly back to Washington to report to my superiors. I'll return here within the next few days, but I doubt you'll need my help in the interrogation. I'm sure you will have persuaded Carr to confess and tell all. Just remember, he can't be killed or seriously injured." Stewart recognized he was taking a risk in revealing his plan to leave Saudi Arabia to the Colonel, but decided it was riskier not to. Al-Saud night well be keeping Stewart under surveillance and would probably have become suspicious and had Stewart arrested if he had attempted to slip out of the country undetected.

After the briefest of goodbyes, the Colonel headed out of the restaurant. Stewart paid the check, then left and walked back to his hotel. Time passed very slowly as he sat in an easy chair and attempted to divert himself by watching an American western movie on the TV.

Finally, about nine, Stewart received the call he had been expecting. Al-Saud informed him that Carr had been taken into custody and transported to the Ulaysha prison. The Colonel recounted with great satisfaction how they had tricked Carr into getting into the car voluntarily, using the pretext that a package addressed to him had arrived opened at the Riyadh post office and that some of the contents had been found to be barred from import into the country. "By the time he realized something was happening," Al-Saud laughed, "He was safely in his cell."

The phone call with the Colonel concluded. Stewart called the Saudi airline to arrange for a seat on the next day's flight back to Washington. It took him some time to get through because of the late hour. When the desk clerk finally came answered, Stewart learned that the flight left at five am., but was all sold out.

Stewart was about to hang up and call Colonel Al-Saud to ask him to use his influence to get him on the flight when the clerk noted that there were first-class seats available on the flight. The CIA officer quickly reserved a first class seat. Leaving a call at the desk to be awakened at three thirty, he hurriedly undressed and got into bed.

Awakened the next morning by his wake-up call, Stewart dressed and went down to the lobby. He checked out and then took cab to the Riyadh airport. He had misjudged the time required to reach the airport and had to rush to make his plane.

Stewart relaxed in his comfortable first-class seat when a horrible thought came to him. Suppose Colonel Al-Saud question Carr about the document Stewart had given him and Carr had told him it was given him by Stewart. Al-Saud might well smell a rat and order Stewart dragged off the plane. He could well image the sort of interrogation the Colonel would employ against him.

When the plane took off, Stewart breathed a sigh of relief. He had left Saudi Arabia; he was safe. His euphoria lasted only a short time before he realized he was on a Saudi plane,. If Al-Saud wished to order it to abort the flight and return to Riyadh, he could do so.

Each hour as the plane headed further from Riyadh and closer to Washington, Stewart tried without success to divert his attention from his risky situation by watching the movies on the cabin screen. It was no use. All he could think of was his being brutally interrogated in the Ulaysha prison.

Finally, the plane passed the half-way point, the point over the Atlantic which Stewart estimated it could not return to Saudi Arabia without refueling. He decided that if the plane made an unscheduled stop in Newfoundland, he would force his way off it and attempt to hide until it took off without him.

When Stewart's plane landed at Washington's Dulles Airport, he breathed a sigh of relief. He was so pleased to be home safely that he felt like kissing the ground beneath him. Clearing customs and immigration without difficulty, he got into a taxi and ordered the driver to take him to the CIA Headquarters.

Stewart arrived at the headquarters building and took an elevator to the floor housing the Mid East Division. He didn't wait to have the secretary buzz Featherstone but walked straight into the Division Chief's office. "Good God," Featherstone said when he saw Stewart, "I didn't expect to see you so soon. Why didn't you cable us? What happened? Were you successful?"

"Yes," Stewart answered, sitting down. "You can start the planning for the military strike immediately. I didn't call you because I didn't want anyone in the Station or Embassy to know what was going on and I obviously couldn't use an open telephone line."

"But what happened? What's the pretext for our attack?" "I arranged for the Saudi Interior Ministry to arrest George Carr, one of the Station communicators. They think Carr is involved in an ISIS plot to assassinate the King. We can now mount a rescue mission. Carr's being held in the Ulaysha Prison, which is close to the Saudi Royal Palace." "I assume that story about Carr is complete fabrication?" Featherstone asked.

"It is," Stewart replied. "I hated to do it. He's a nice kid. I tried to protect him as far as I could by telling the Saudi's that he couldn't be killed or seriously injured." I think they got the message.

"Let's hope so," the Division Chief said grimly. "We'd better inform the Deputy Director." When they arrived at Chapman's office, the latter echoed Featherstone's surprise at seeing Stewart back so quickly. At Featherstone's suggestion, Stewart explained what he had accomplished in Riyadh. When Stewart had finished, Chapman sat quietly, looking at him. "Is that all?he asked."

Stewart stared at him surprised. "I beg your pardon, sir?'

The Deputy Director returned the stare. "I appreciate," he said, "That you were given an impossible mission. But frankly all you've accomplished is getting one of the Riyadh Station communicators jailed and presumably now undergoing torture. How does that accomplish want the President wants?"

Stewart realized Chapman had not fully understood what he was suggesting. "What I should have made clearer," he said, "Was that what I've just told you has nothing to do with the President's request. Carr, an American diplomat, has been arrested on bogus charges that he is an ISIS agent planning to assassinate the King. He is being held in the Ulaysha Prison and being tortured by the Saudi's in attempt to force him to reveal our codes. If he is broken, all Embassy traffic and possibly all American diplomatic traffic will be open to the Saudi's and anyone else they choose to share it with."

"The Prison," Stewart continued, "Is located near the Royal Palace in area area heavily defended by missile batteries and other anti-aircraft installations. It will require heavy Air Force bombers to neutralized the installations. It is even conceivable that a few bombs may miss their target and destroy the Royal Palace."

The Deputy Director nodded in agreement. "There You're right. We may have to act to get Carr released. It's something I'll have to take to the Director for his approval." He stood. "Let's go now," he said.

The other two rose as well. "If you don't need me now," Featherstone said, "I'll go back to my office. He made no effort to disguise his desire to stay as far away from the enterprise as possible. As he headed for the door, Chapman made no effort to stop him. "Come with me," he said to Stewart led the way to the elevator to the Director's office.

When they reached Collins' office, his secretary buzzed the Director and quickly ushered them in. Collins looked at Chapman inquiringly. "It's about that Saudi matter," Chapman began."

Collins stared at him angrily. "I told you I didn't want to know anything about it," he said. "You know what has to be done.! Do it!."

Chapman met his eyes and did not back down. "I'm afraid I have to talk to you about this," he said. "Stewart here has arranged for us to do what is necessary, but the orders have to come from you. If I tried to issue them, I'd be told I didn't have the authority."

"All right," Collins said. "Just remember, this meeting never took place."

Chapman turned to the desk chief. "Explain it to him, Tom."

"this conversation has nothing to do with the President," Stewart began. It's solely about the arrest and torture by the Saudi's of George Carr, a Station communicator." He repeated what he had told to Chapman. When he had finished, Collins smiled.

"Fine, he said, "Get on with it. You have my authorization for a military raid to free Carr, using whatever means may be necessary."

"This is something that has to go to the President," Chapman told him.

"Why? he doesn't want to be involved."

Stewart and Chapman stared at each other. The Deputy Director realized that Stewart was too overawed to try and convince Collins. He would have to do it himself. "Sir," he said, "To knock out the Saudi anti-aircraft installations defending the prison we need the Air Force. The Agency does not have that kind of a military capability. Beyond that, our Special Operations people don't have the heavy weapons needed to overwhelm the Saudi Interior Ministry force protecting the prison. I estimate we would need a team of about forty, made up of Navy Seals and Army Rangers. Finally, it would be better for the Agency if we are not publicly identified with this operation. It would facilitate our re-establishing close relations with the Saudi Security forces, which we will almost certainly desire."

Collins nodded. "Those are good reasons. The problem is convincing the President. We're awfully close to the next election."

A horrible image flashed across Stewart's mind of George Carr being brutally tortured in the cellars of the Ulaysha Prison due solely to his actions in Riyadh. "Mr. Director," he broke in almost shouting, "The President has to take action! If on top of the Saudi cutting off of the West's oil supplies they seize and torture an American diplomat and the U.S. does nothing, he'll lose the election in a landslide."

Chapman was about to rebuke Stewart for his comments when Collins interrupted. "You may be right young man. I'm going over to the White House to try and sell them on your plan. Stay close in case I have to call you for any details. Chapman and Stewart left and the Director had his secretary call to arrange an immediate meeting for him with the President's National Security Adviser.

When Chapman and Stewart left Collin's office, the Deputy Director returned to his own and Stewart stopped off to brief Featherstone on the meeting with the Director. Stewart found Featherstone in a gloomy state of mind. "I don't like it," he said, "It's a bad plan. Too many things can go wrong. I'm not blaming you, you did what you were told. What Chapman and I should have done was tell Collins we wouldn't accept the President's order, that it was illegal. If necessary, we should have resigned. Some things are important enough to give up a job for."

Stewart was uncertain as to how to respond. He limited himself to saying a simple, "Yes, sir." Back in his own office, Stewart sat at his desk, his mind too filled with the events of the last few days to be able to work.

Collins, meanwhile. Finally go through to Hunter. It took him considerable time, but he finally managed to obtain the National security Adviser's agreement to include Collins on his schedule that day. The CIA Director left his office and had his driver take him to the White House. He then spent the next two hours sitting in Hunter's outer office as the latter participated in one meeting after another.

When Collins was finally ushered in to Hunter's office the National Security Adviser apologized for keeping him waiting. "The North Koreans are threatening the South again," he said, "And we had to work out instructions to our Navy vessels in the area. Now what was the urgent matter you said you had to discuss with me?"

The CIA Director laid out in detail the scenario designed by Stewart for the military strike on Riyadh designed to eliminate the King. When he had finished, Hunter's first question was "Can you guarantee this plan will work?"

Collins thought for a minute. He realized that if he said yes and he was wrong, the President would immediately fire him. On the other hand, his failure to fulfill the President's directive would also result in his removal. "Dick," he answered. "I can't guarantee it will work. Something can always go wrong. But I estimate the chances of success as about eighty percent."

Hunter shrugged. "I guess we'll have to go with it then. I'll take it to the President as soon as I can get in to see him. I should be able to get back to you before midnight." Collins said goodbye and went back down to where his car was parked for the return to CIA Headquarters.

For the rest of the afternoon, Collins, Chapman and Stewart sat in their respective offices awaiting word from the White House on the President's decision. It finally came shortly after eight pm, when Hunter called the CIA Director to inform him Baker had given his go-ahead on the plan. "The Secretary of Defense will be the lead person on the project;

you are to contact Secretary Kincade and inform him of the Agency official who will work with him. Everything has to be ready within a week. The President plans to go on nation-wide TV a few minutes before the strike on Riyadh to inform the public of the need for the attack."

"One more thing," the National Security Adviser continued, "The President wanted me to impress on you the necessity that the death of the King look like an accident. Do you understand?"

When Collins hung up, he sat back and thought over how best to carry out the President's instructions. His first decision was to have the Deputy Director for Operations act as the Agency's lead with the Defense Department. The CIA Director was aware that anything went wrong with Stewart's scenario, he would almost certainly be dragged down. Nevertheless, if there was any possibility of isolating himself from a failure, it would be foolish to disregard it.

Collins next called Chapman and told him he would be the Agency official responsible for coordinating with the Defense Department on the Saudi project. He stressed the priority for the King's death to appear accidental and the short time limit. "The Deputy Director," he added, should draw upon Featherstone and Stewart's assistance as required."

The Deputy Director cursed under his breath at Collin's instructions. He had been hoping that good sense would prevail in the White House and that Stewart's plan would be rejected. It had been a long and stressful day and he wanted nothing so much as to close up his office and go home. He knew, however, that Featherstone and Stewart were still in their offices awaiting his call. In good conscience, there was nothing he could do but summon them up to see him.

When his two subordinates arrived, Chapman informed them of Collin's orders to him. The Middle East Division Chief was the first to speak. "I don't like it," he said. "Too much could go wrong. The Saudi's could shoot down the helicopters carrying our rescue force, the bombers could miss the palace, the King might not e in the Palace when we bomb it. I'm afraid all we're going to do is get Carr killed and the Saudi's declare a holy war against us. "

"All right," the Deputy Director answered. "What do you propose we do. We have the President's order. We have no choice but to obey it."

"I think," Featherstone said, " It's our responsibility to go back and tell them it's not an order we can or should carry out. If necessary, I'm ready to resign."

"What do you think Tom?" Chapman asked the desk chief.

"Joe is correct, Stewart answered. "It's a bad plan. A lot could go wrong. It's simply the least bad alternative we have if we to are to carry out the President's order. There is no alternative. We can't leave Carr to be tortured by the Saudi's."

Chapman remained silent for a few minutes. "I think Tom is right," he said finally "We can't allow Carr to rot. And, if we resigned, Collins would simply replacement us with people who would carry out the President's orders."

Looking at the angry expression on Featherstone's face, Chapman added, "Joe, don't do anything foolish. You're doing a great job running the Division and I don't want to lose you. It's been a long day," he added, "Let's go home."

As Featherstone and Stewart stood, Chapman was about to tell them to report to his office on the following day to coordinate the Agency role in the Saudi operation. One look at Featherstone's face convinced him that would be a bad idea. Recalling that Stewart had come directly to the Agency from the airport and probably did not have his car in the lot, Chapman asked the Desk Chief if he needed a ride to his home. Stewart gratefully accepted.

During the short drive to Stewart's house, Stewart and Chapman discussed the Saudi project. As he got out of the car, Deputy Director expressed his sincere gratitude to desk chief. "I hope you realize," he added, "Just how valuable your work has been.

Stewart walked up to his house in a a happy mood. With Chapman's backing, his future in the Agency was assured. Quite possibly, when Featherstone left the Division for his next assignment, Stewart might be moved up to replace him.

The house was silent as Stewart entered. He climbed the stairs and found Mary in bed, correcting papers. "Hi dear," he said, "I'm home."

She looked up astonished as h e walked over and hugged her. "I missed you terribly." he whispered.

"Me, too," she answered. "But how did you get back so soon? Did everything go well?"

"I'm not sure. But at least I'm home." He was about to tell her about his trip and then decided against it. There was no sense in worrying her.

"Have you had supper? Can I get you something to eat?"

Stewart realized he was famished. "I'd love something, if it's not too much trouble."

Mary got out of bed and went down to the kitchen, where he could hear her working. He stripped, took a warm shower and put on his pajamas. He heard her call him to say dinner was ready and he went downstairs to join her.

The next morning Stewart drove to the Agency and went up to Chapman's office. For the rest of the day Stewart and the Deputy Director worked on the attack plan. They were in almost hourly communication with the Defense Department to integrate their information with that of the military's. Particular attention was given to disguising the fact that the coordinates of the anti-aircraft installations which were to be struck actually include those of the Royal Palace.

Despite constant goading from the White House, preparations for the attack consumed eight days. The Defense Department suggested including Stewart in the rescue force to ensure that there was someone familiar with the layout of the prison and capable of identifying Carr. Chapman vetoed this, stressing that if he were on the scene the Saudis would have definite proof of the Agency's involvement in the scheme.

President Baker's televised speech to the nation on the crisis with Saudi Arabia was carefully worded. It did not specify what action the United States would take if Saudi

Arabia "Did not immediately free George Carr." It also was timed to avoid giving the Saudi's time to prepare for any attack. The American planes were already overflying Saudi Arabia by the time he concluded his speech and the bombers struck the Palace and the Riyadh air defenses within minutes.

Collins, Chapman and Stewart had gathered in the CIA Operations Center to follow the operation. They were aided by receipt of radio reports from the helicopters carrying the landing party. In all there were six helicopters carrying the Army Rangers and Navy Seals assigned to free Carr plus and additional four helicopter gunships to provide close air support for the landing party.

Collins, Chapman, Featherstone and Stewart were joined in the crowded Operations Center by other CIA officials eager to minute-by-minute information on the attack. As they listened the assault party disembarked safely from the helicopters and stormed the Ulaysha Prison. Despite the attackers' advantage of initiative and heavier weapons, the prison guards put up a fierce resistance, with almost a dozen of the American force being killed or wounded before all resistance ceased.

The cell housing Carr was located after some delay and the captive American was aided to reach the helicopter that would bear him to safety. Next loaded were the wounded and the bodies of the dead, followed by the rear guard of the landing force.

An air of accomplishment and near-euphoria permeated the Operations Center as the six helicopters took off safely.

Suddenly, several loud crashes were heard followed by shouts of "We've been hit!" Next came a near hysterical transmission from one of the helicopters: "(Copters two and three have crashed. Give us covering fire! We're landing to rescue survivors!"

Subsequent messages reported that all of the passengers on Copter number two had been killed in the crash, including George Carr. Several of the occupants of Copter three were injured, with one fatality. The survivors of the crashes loaded on other copters, then entire force headed as rapidly as possible to exit Saudi air space. Amid the gloom that permeated the Operations Center, Collins instructed all Agency communications monitoring stations to report on the effects of the bombing and whether the King had been killed or injured. In a more guarded cable, he cabled the Riyadh Station, requesting an immediate and detailed report on the Saudi Government's reactions.

For the next three days, Collins waited to be summoned to the White House to submit his resignation as Director. The rescue mission had obviously been a disaster. Not only had two of the helicopters been shot down with loss of American life, but the ostensible purpose for the attack, freeing Carr, had culminated in the communication officer's death. Even more important, the Saudi broadcasts reported the King carrying out his normal duties. Riyadh Station confirmed his survival of the bomb attack on the palace.

The CIA Director could gather no hint of his fate from the administration's public utterances on the raid. The White House Press Secretary's terse announcements said only that

U.S. Forces had succeeded in securing the release of the American state Department official illegally held captive in Saudi Arabia. In response to a reporter's question, the Spokesman had admitted that there had been "a couple of injured as a result of a crash on the return flight."

On the fourth day after the attack, the Cabinet held its regular weekly session. The CIA Director entered the Cabinet room and took his customary seat, conscious of being the center of attention. Glancing at the agenda, he saw that there was no item dealing with the attack.

"Let's begin," the President said. "Before we get into the items on the agenda, I'm happy to report that relations with Saudi Arabia are back on track. The Saudi Foreign Minister informed our Ambassador today that the King has rejected suggestions from his Oil Ministry to increase the price oil and to replace Western oil technicians with those from Russia."

There were a few expressions of pleasure from those sitting around the table, but no one deemed it opportune to comment further on the Riyadh attack. The items on the agenda were covered one by one, with Collins not feeling inclined to speak. At the meeting's close, the CIA Director stood and turned toward the door. He heard his name called behind him and turned to see the National Security Adviser beckoning him to approach.

"Can you come to my office for a few minutes,? Hunter asked. The two chatted as they walked to the Security Adviser's office and sat down. Collins was sure that the moment he had dreaded had arrived and that Hunter would convey the President's demand he immediately resign. Startled, the CIA Director heard Hunter say "The President asked me to congratulate you and the Agency for the way you supported the attack on Riyadh. Although," he continued, "There was collateral damage, that was to be expected. "

Collins breathed a sigh of relief. "I'll pass that word back to the Agency."

"There's one more thing," Hunter went on. "The President wanted me to stress to you the absolute necessity for the Agency's role to remain secret."

"But it is," the CIA Director protested. "

"Who knows about it?"

"Well, Collins began, "The work in Riyadh was handled by Tom Stewart, the Saudi Desk Chief. He deserves most of the credit."

He was interrupted by Hunter. "He's got to be be eliminated."

"What?"

Hunter repeated, "He's got to be eliminated. It can't be helped."

The CIA Director stared at him. "Are you really suggesting killing him? Stewart's one of our best officers."

"There's no alternative. Nothing about the attack can get out. Stewart is too big a risk."

Collins thought about refusing the order. He hesitated, then decided against it. In part, sixteen months in the

Director's job, during which time he had routinely accepted the most inane orders from the White House, had eroded his will-power. And, he told himself, if he refused and were fired, whomever the White House chose to replace him could easily learn about Chapman's participation and decide to eliminate Chapman as well.

Collins shrugged. "All right," he said, "I'll take care of it.

Back in his office, the CIA Director summoned Chapman and Featherstone. He did not take the time to offer them a cup of coffee but launched into his subject immediately. "I saw the President's National Security Adviser today. We've got trouble."

"We're all fired and the Agency disbanded?" Chapman asked with gallows humor.

"No, nothing like that, the Director answered. "In fact, the President was pleased by the operation. The Saudi King was apparently sufficiently intimidated by the raid to cancel his plans to hit the West on oil. The President has me to convey his gratitude to the Agency for our work in supporting the Defense Department in preparing for the attack."

"What's the trouble, then? "Chapman inquired. "It seems we've ended up smelling like a rose."

"I'm afraid not," Collins explained. "He now wants all the 'loose ends' cleaned up.."

"What loose ends?" Chapman asked. " There aren't any. Only Stewart knows the details and he certainly won't talk."

"I'm afraid the White House doesn't agree with you," the Director came back in a low voice. "Hunter told me to specifically to liquidate Stewart. He asked me who knew about the work in Riyadh and I gave Stewart the credit. I thought he deserved recognition. Fortunately, he interrupted me for I could mention you, Ross They way he was going, he probably would have put you on the list as well."

"You can't be serious Chapman said. The White House couldn't be that stupid."

"I'm afraid they are."

"I hope you refused."

"I thought about it," Collins said. "I decided it wouldn't do any good. They'd simply replace me with someone who would and who might put us on the target list."

Featherstone, who had been sitting quietly during the conversation, broke in. "I won't condone in Tom's murder," he said. "I'm prepared to resign on the spot and go public. That monster in the White House has to be stopped. "I m ready to go to the "New York Times" and the TV networks if I have to."

Chapman nodded. "I agree with Joe. If he leaves, I'll go with him."

The CIA Director realized that both his subordinates were serious. If they went public about the White House, it would destroy not only the administration but also the Agency. And, in part he agreed with them. "All right," he said, "I'll find some alternative."

"I want your word of honor," Featherstone insisted, "that Tom wont be killed."

"You have it," the CIA Director said, shaking hands with Chapman and Featherstone.

"What will you do?" The Deputy Director asked.

"I'll manage to work something out. You can go now. I'll take care of it. But for God's sake keep your heads down. We've got to get off the White House radar if I'm to save Stewart."

As they left the Director's office and walked back downstairs, Featherstone asked, "Ross, can be trust Collins to keep his word?"

"I'm sure we can," Chapman answered. "He always keeps his word." Back in his own office, the Deputy Director thought about his answer to Featherstone and wondered if he still believed it.

In his office, Collins sat back and wondered how he could honor his commitment to Featherstone and Chapman while still satisfying the White House's demand to liquidate all loose ends. He thought back to his youth, when for a time he had considered becoming a priest. This led him to ponder of the great French statesman Cardinal Richelieu had been able to satisfy his conscience while administering the affairs of state.

Under normal circumstances, as Director Collins would have assigned Chapman the task of handling the matter of Stewart. Now, the Deputy Director would be of no use. Then, getting an idea, he buzzed his secretary and told her "Please have Dr. Steiner come to my office."

A short time later, there was a know on his door and Dr. Fritz Steiner entered. He was a physician with the CIA Medical Services Division assigned to provide close support to the Operations Directorate.

"Dr. Steiner," Collins began, "The Agency has a problem in which I'd like your assistance. We have someone who has unfortunately come into the possession of information too dangerous for the country to have him retain. We don't wish to kill him. We don't want to ill him. Is there any way of removing the specific memory from his mind while harming him as little as possible?"

The doctor thought for a minute and asked, 'When did he learn this information? How long ago?"

"Less than a month. Would the exact date help?"

"No, there is no need to be more precise. There are two methods, Dr. Steiner said slowly. One chemical the other surgical. With the chemical method the target is injected or preferably consumes a liquid which alters his mind. His thinking process is seriously compromised and the subject can end up anything from a helpless idiot to someone who is of low average intelligence.

Collins shuddered at the thought of someone like Stewart being reduced to the state of a helpless idiot. "I'd hate to do that," he said, "What's the other way?"

The surgical method has the disadvantage of requiring physical control of the subject. Do we have that?" "I think that can be arranged," Collins answered. "What is the time period required?"

"Approximately a week in the hospital. Of course, he would then require a period of rest and recovery at home before he could resume regular activities."

"That seems to be the way to go then," the Director said. "How soon can you make the arrangements."

Probably in about a week. However, you should understand that this is an experimental procedure and success cannot be guaranteed."

"You mean he may die?" Collins asked.

"No, nothing like that. But it can result in complete amnesia, the patient not knowing his own identity. Or he may lose his knowledge of a particular language or know who he is but not recognize close family members."

"I understand," Collins said gravely. "Well, if that's the only choice, we have to do it. Start now."

"One more detail," Steiner added. "The procedure has to be done at a first rate hospital. Some place like Johns Hopkins or New York Presbyterian."

The Director shook his head. "It's impossible for security reasons for the procedure to be performed in the US. It would be best if we could do it somewhere in Eastern Europe. Are there any hospitals in Poland that would qualify?"

Steiner thought for a minute before answering. Then he said, "We might be able to make due in Warsaw. I don't think there's any surgeon in Warsaw skilled enough in the technique, but I believe I can bring in someone from Vienna who would be permitted to operate in Warsaw."

The Director nodded. "Good. Let's do it."

After the doctor left, Collins had his secretary obtain Stewart's personnel file. He read it thoroughly to learn the details of Stewart's service. After he used the information he had collected to prepare a credible story to give the Saudi desk chief as a reason to send him to Warsaw, Collins turned to obtaining the required support from Polish security officials.

The Director had never served in Poland and had never met the head of the Polish Service. He began by instructing his secretary to bring him the latest four reports from the Chief of Station in Warsaw. These reports, which were sent to him from every CIA Station in the world monthly, were supposed to describe the operating environment in the station, notable events, successes, and problems. He found what he needed, mention in one report information provided the Station by HYSPOON -4, the alias given a valuable asset in the Polish Security Service.

Collins called the Polish Desk Chief and told him to send up to his office the dossier of HYSPOON-4 and the personal file of the Station case officer handling him. Reading the agent's file careful, the Director decided HYSPOON-4 would be a likely choice to handle the Warsaw operation. Alan Harrington, the case officer, seemed a competent officer and capable of performing the limited role Collins had in mind for him.

His plan completed, the Director began to put it into action. He would have preferred to go directly to Warsaw to meet with Harrington. He decided, however, that it would be foolish to risk drawing attention to HYSPOON-4 by visiting the Polish capital. Instead, he sent a personal cable to the Chief of Station Warsaw instructing him to send Harrington to Berlin to meet with a "Mr. Brown" in the Intercontinental Hotel. The case officer was to rent a room in the hotel and remain there until contacted by Brown.

After sending the cable, Collins had to wait to hear from Dr. Steiner that he had located the required brain surgeon. It required two days before the physician came to Collins' office to tell him he had been successful. "I've been able to persuade one of the finest surgeons in Germany to do the job, " he said with a smile. "Dr. doctor Conrad Mueller. I gave him a cock and bull story which he pretended to believe. One advantage is that he has performed brain surgery previously n the Grotski Institute in Warsaw and will have no problem using it now for the patient you want. He's demanded a fee of a hundred thousand dollars in a numbered Swiss bank account. I assumed you'd agree."

The Director nodded. "Yes, of course. It's not as though we have much choice. Good work, Doctor. How soon can we get him to Warsaw for the operation?"

"Mueller said he can make it to Warsaw by the end of the week."

"Fine," Collins said. "Give him the go-ahead for the end of the week. We'll have our patient at the Grotski Institute ready for him."

After the doctor left, Collins made his arrangements to fly to Berlin. To reduce the chance of his being recognized, he would travel in alias as "Mr. Brown," and disguise himself with a false beard.

The Director rarely took vacations and enjoyed the opportunity to relax during the flight to Berlin, watching the movies on the cabin screen. He took a taxi from the airport to the Intercontinental Hotel, registered and inquired if his friend, Alan Harrington, had already arrived. He was relived to learn that the case officer was already there and obtained his room number.

Collins was led to his room and, as soon as the bellhop had departed called Harrington's room. When the phone was answered he asked, "Alan Harrington?"

"Yes,."

"This is is Mr. Brown, Can you please come to room 423 now."

"I'll be right there."

After a short interval, there was a know on the door and Collins opened it to find a pleasant looking young man facing him. "Come in Mr. Harrington," he said, shaking Harrington's hand. This is my passport, he added, showing the passport identifying him as Robert Brown. "Could I see your passport please."

The case officer looked surprised at the precaution, but quickly confirmed his identity by showing his own passport to the Director. "Thank you," Collins told him. "Please sit down."

"As you probably surmise," the Director began, ""You've been ordered here to participate in an especially sensitive operation. You have been selected because of your fine handling of HYCHAIR-4 and the access he can provide. I gathered from the file that you recruited him. Is this correct?'

"Yes, sir. That is, I recruited him to be a unilateral agent, reporting to us on the activities of the Polish Service. Before that he was a liaison contact, providing only that information his Service authorized him to transmit."

"What was his motivation in accepting recruitment?" Collins asked.

"In part money. But I found him to be quite pro-American. In fact, I've had to caution him to conceal his pro-American sentiments. Although most of the strongly anti-American officers have left the Polish Service by this time, if he shows he is pro-American, it could sharply limit his access to information of use to us".

Harrington's description of the agent's pro-American proclivities was welcome news to the Director. He had been planning to take the risk of traveling to Warsaw with the case officer to meet HYCHAIR-4 and personally supervise the operation. Based on this new information, he decided return to Washington, assigning to the case officer the job of supervising HYCHAIR-4's role.

"You understand," the Director began, "That what I am about to tell you is highly confidential. It must never be repeated to anyone, not even to your chief in Warsaw. All you tell him about your stay in Berlin is that you met with Mr. Brown, who spoke with you on a highly-classified matter."

When Harrington answered,"Yes, sir,." the Director went on. " We have learned that an individual using the name of Charles Rice has stolen the top secret details of America's missile defense system in Europe. He is offering to sell them to the Russians. If he succeeds, our missile defense system can be rendered useless. It is essential that he be prevented from turning the plans over."

"That is serious," Harrington agreed. "What would you like me to do?"

"Rice will be in Zakopane at the Nosalowy Dwor resort. That's the Polish ski resort in southern Poland near the Slovakian border."

"Yes, I know," Harrington said. "I skied there once."

"Good, Collins answered. "Then you're generally familiar with the layout of the town. But you must understand, you must not go there yourself. Everything has to be handled by HYCHAIR-4. We need him to take Rice into custody there and transport him to Warsaw to the Grotski Institute. We have arranged to use that facility to interrogate him. Since it is a medical facility, we have to disguise Rice to look like a patient."

Collins stopped to make sure that the case officer was taking this all in. Satisfied, he continued, "Rice should not be aware as to what is going on. He should be lured into a car on some excuse, then put to sleep with chloroform or something similar. We don't want him hit on the head with a blackjack or injured in any way. Once unconscious, his head must be wrapped in bandages to simulate a head injury and he be transported to the Institute in Warsaw by ambulance."

The Director had Harrington repeat the instructions to him and was pleased that the case officer had grasped the elements of the plan. "Do you foresee any difficulties in persuading HYCHAIR-4 to conduct the operation? You can offer him as large a bonus as is necessary."

"No, it should be easy. I may mention the cash, but I don't believe it will be necessary. I will tell him its equally important to Poland as to the United States because of the risk Rice constitutes for our anti-missile defenses. The Poles are so frightened on Russia right now that the Polish Government would almost certainly agree to grab rice for us if we requested them. However. That would take more time to obtain their agreement than we have available."

Collins was impressed by the young case officer's astuteness. "You may be sure," he said "That the Director will be informed of your role in this operation. If you bring it off successfully, the fact will be reported to the next promotion board with the recommendation that you receive promotion."

Harrington smiled. "I'll make it successful, or I'll die trying."

After the Director bid Harrington goodbye and watched him depart, he checked out of the hotel and had a taxi drive him to the airport. Securing a seat on the next flight back to Washington, he remained apprehensive over the outcome of the operation. Despite the most meticulous planning, too much could go wrong.

Back in his office the next day, Collins sent for Dr. Steiner to tell him the operation was on track. Sounding more confident than he felt, the Director said that the subject would be delivered to the Grotski Institute by ambulance the coming Saturday, his head wrapped in bandages to create the impression of a skull injury and heavily sedated. Dr. Mueller was to operate as soon as possible thereafter and to immediately notify Steiner of the outcome of the operation. "Other than to ensure the subject's condition and the success of the operation in removing recent memories, the subject should not be questioned further. To the extent necessary to prevent him from speaking to other persons, he should be tranquilized or his mouth covered with bandages to prevent speaking."

Dr. Steiner signified his understanding. As a physician, he was disturbed by the treatment the subject was to receive, but reluctantly accepted its necessity for the national interest of the U.S.

The next step for Collins was to get Stewart to the Nosalowy Dwor Ski resort in Zakopane in place to be grabbed by HYCHAIR-4. He asked his secretary to have Stewart come immediately to his office. Stewart entered, a worried expression on his face. He considered his mission in Riyadh to

141

have been a disastrous failure, with the King emerging unhurt and Carr dead.

"Congratulations, " Collins said to the bewildered desk chief, "On your success in Riyadh. The President has expressed to me his great pleasure in the way things worked out, with Saudi Arabia completing reversing its oil plans."

"Thank you, sir," Stewart replied, uncertain about whether to voice his worry over Carr's death."

"You did so well, " Collins continued, "That I have another special mission for you. I want you to go to Poland. We have a sensitive asset you will meet there, at the Nosalowy Dwor Ski resort in Zakopane. He is traveling under the alias of Banet. You will travel under the alias of Charles Rice. He will contact you in your room at the Ski Resort, probably on this Saturday. You will wait there until he arrives. Is that understood?"

"Yes, sir," Said Stewart, swallowing his disappointment. He had hopped he would be able to take Mary and his children to the beach for a vacation..

When Stewart left, the Director called the CIA Cover Staff and instructed them to prepare a false passport for the Saudi desk chief in the name of Charles Rice. He thought for a minute and told them to make it an official passport rather than a diplomatic one. With an official passport, it would be easier to bring Stewart back to Washington. If Stewart were traveling with a diplomatic passport, there was too much chance the U.S. Embassy in Warsaw would become involved in the case.

For the following three days, Collins tried to carry out his regular responsibilities, but found it impossible to shut the Stewart case out of his mind. On Saturday he came in early as usual. He constantly checked his watch to calculate what time it was in Warsaw. He was joined in the early afternoon by Dr. Steiner. Together, they waited for a call from Dr. Mueller reporting on the results of the operation.

When they had heard nothing by six pm., Collins told Steiner to telephone the Grotski Institute and inquire about Stewart's condition. Steiner was told only that Dr. Mueller was still in the operating room and that no information on the patient's condition was available. Finally after nine, the phone rang and Dr. Mueller reported that the patient had survived the surgery and had now been taken out of the recovery room. As to the state of his memory, no concrete reading would be available for at least twenty-four hours. With receipt of the news, Collins and Steiner felt free to leave Collin's office and return to their respective homes.

It was with the greatest of relief that the Director received Mueller's next phone call. The doctor sounded pleased as he reported that Rice was now conscious and responding rationally to simple questions. The only difficulty he experienced was confusion about his name, insisting it was Tom Stewart instead of the Charles Rice.

Collins smiled as he heard this. Clearly , from the operation had been successful, removing from Stewart's brain the memory of the Saudi operation. Mueller further reported that Stewart could safely be discharged from the Institute to travel back to the United States in a few days if accompanied by an escort and on a direct flight. He would, however, require a lengthy period of convalescence, either at home or in some type of sanitarium.

Finding a suitable place for Stewart was not difficult. The CIA had been given a large Maryland estate not from from Washington, equipped with tennis courts and swimming pool. Normally it was used to interrogate high-level Russian defectors or as the site for senior seminars. The Director ordered that it be readied to receive Stewart and that medial personnel from the Agency's Medical Division be assigned there to take care of the desk chief.

Collins next turned his attention to bringing Stewart back to the US. He contacted the Security Division and asked them to send to his office two Security Officers whom he had used previously and found efficient. When they arrived he instructed them to fly to Warsaw to pick up at the Grotski Institute a patient registered there as Charles Rice. Rice was to be escorted back to Washington on the next available first class. No comment should be made to the patient if he called himself Tom Stewart, He also should be prevented from speaking to anyone other to the extent possible. Collins explained this as due to the fact that Rice was still disoriented due to a recent head injury.

Several days after Stewart's safe arrival at the estate, Collins had his car drive him to visit Stewart. He found the desk chief sitting up in bed reading. "Good morning, Tom," he said, "how are you feeling?"

The answer, "Fine thanks," was automatic , but at least the voice sounded normal.

"I'm Jim Collins, the Agency Director." Collins continued. "Do you remember meeting me?"

"No, sir, although you do look familiar. But as far as I know, the Director is Admiral Porter."

This was the best answer Stewart could have given Collins. Admiral Porter had been his predecessor as CIA Director. As confirmation, he asked Stewart what his last assignment had been. "Why as a Case Officer in Riyadh for the last two years," was the answer. This was solid proof that Stewart's inconvenient memories had been removed from his brain and that he had no knowledge of his time as Saudi desk chief. For how long was of course a question. For Stewart's own safety and possible for Collins' safety as well it had to last until the Baker administration was no longer in office.

Pleased with his visit to see Stewart, Collins returned to his office feeling greatly relieved. The awful burden of dealing with the President's illegal orders to first liquidate the Saudi King and then Stewart seemed to have been satisfactorily resolved. He was happily doing his usual work when his secretary buzzed to say that Chapman and Featherstone were in his office and wishing see him.

As soon as they entered and been seated than the Middle East Division Chief blurted out, "What's happened to Tom Stewart? You promised us he wouldn't be killed. He's been out of the office for two weeks, without anyone hearing from him. When I called his wife, Mary told me he had left on some sort of operational mission and she had not hear from him. All I can assume is that you lied to us and he's dead."

Collins looked at Chapman and saw the Deputy Director agreed with his subordinate. It was also clear that only the truth or something approximating the truth would persuade them to avoid an open controversy, destroying the administration and quite likely the Agency.

"All right," he said, I can see I'm going to have to give you some information which will be extremely dangerous to you to possess. Do I have your word that you will never discuss what I am about to tell you to anyone, not even each other."

Both Chapman and Featherstone solemnly pledged their silence.

"Please understand. After I have finished, you are not to ask any further questions. Against the President's orders, Tom Stewart is still alive. He was on a secret mission abroad and was injured. He was taken to a medical facility where there was a brain operation resulting in a partial loss of memory. He is now back in the US and recovering. I visited him a few days ago and found him up in bed reading. He knows his own name but has suffered a partial loss of memory, for how long it is impossible to predict. He remembered he had seen me previous, but thought that the CIA Director is still Admiral Porter and has no memory of his work as Saudi Desk Chief."

"I've placed Stewart on a year's full pay to rest and recuperate," Collins added. "At the end of that time, if its safe and his physical condition permits he will be returned to a good job. If not, he'll receive a full retirement as though he had completed twenty years of service .I will also will also call Mary and offer her and the children the opportunity to vacation with him for as long as they wish at the place he is staying, which has a swimming pool and tennis court for them to enjoy. If you wish to see him that can be arranged, but it would be very dangerous to his survival as well as our own. Do you insist on seeing him?"

Chapman quickly answered, "No. We won't expose Tom to any more danger. Come on, Ross," he said standing. "We've learned what we needed. Let's go." Somewhat reluctantly, Featherstone rose and followed the Deputy Director out of the office.

Saudi Arabia was not mentioned by any of the participants at the next session of the Cabinet, leading Collins to conclude that the White House was no longer interested in the subject. He was surprised when, two days after the meeting, he received a call from Hunter. The National Security Adviser invited him to lunch the following day in a manner which left him aware it was an order and not an invitation.

The lunch was at the Hawthorne Club, probably the most prestigious dining club in the capital. It was located on F Street, not from from the Executive Office Building. Collins had briefly considered applying for membership in the club after his appoint as CIA Director, deciding against it because of the steep initiation fee and annual dues. It was his understanding that only those government officials with an independent income could afford to belong; the costs were too heavy for anyone dependent on a government salary to afford.

Collins had his car drop him a few blocks short of the Hawthorne Club and walked the rest of the way. The precaution was probably not necessary, but it was in accordance with his training and it might be better to avoid spectators to his meeting with the National Security Adviser. Collins entered the club stared around him and was impressed. The building dated back to the late nineteenth century and the furnishing resembled what Collins would have expected to find in one of the millionaire's mansions of the Gilded Age.

The maitre d' led him back to enclave in which Hunter was sitting. Crystal chandeliers sparkled from the ceiling and large oil paintings adorned the walls. Collins found the National Security Adviser alone at his table, sipping at a drink.

"Glad you could make it," Hunter said, "Can I order you a drink?"

Collins generally preferred not to drink at lunch. To avoid appearing unfriendly, he answered "I'll have whatever you're drinking," and in a minute was served a glass of fine scotch and soda. "I've already ordered," Hunter said handing him the menu. The waiter recommended duck in orange sauce, which I decided to try. I understand it is one of the chef's specialties."

Once again, Collins followed his host's lead. Waiting for the main dish to be served and then while eating, Collins and Hunter discussed a wide range of national security problems, the CIA Director giving his assessments on the issues raised.

They had reached the desert course before the National Security Adviser broached what Collins assumed was the reason for the meeting.

"President Baker" he began, "Instructed me to make certain that all of the loose ends from that Saudi operation have been cleaned up . Is that correct?"

"Why, of course," Collins replied. "I thought you knew that. I didn't submit any formal confirmation because of what I assumed was the need for secrecy."

"That Saudi desk chief, Tom Stewart, liquidated."

"Yes," Collins answered smoothly, his expression and voice carefully controlled. He had had in his career considerable need to lie effectively and never did so well as with the National Security Adviser now. He acted as though his life depended on it, realizing that it probably did.

After some further desultory conversation, Collins glanced at his watch and saw it was the time he had instructed his driver to pick him up. Standing, he said, "Dick, I apologize for breaking this up but I have to leave now. It was very kind of you to invite me here. It was one of the best meals I've ever had."

The National Security Adviser hastily stood and shook Collins' hand. "I'm very glad you were able to join me. This has been a most interesting and useful conversation. I hope you can make it again soon. I'll call you."

Collins said goodbye and walked toward the exist. Leaving the Hawthorne Club he turned down F Street to where his driver was waiting for him.

After Collins had left, Hunter st down, removed a container from his jacket pocket and opened it., Carefully extracting a final Havana cigar, he lit it, put it in his mouth and puffed contentedly. It was against the rules to smoke in the club, but he knew no one would think of mentioning that to him.

All things considered, he decided the meeting with the CIA Director had gone well. He would now be able to tell the President that all loose ends from the Saudi operation had been cleaned up and particularly that the Saudi desk officer had been eliminated.

Hunter was in full agreement with the President that it was always foolish to permit loose ends. That, of course, raised the question of Collins. He had performed as well as could have been expected and shown both ability and, what was more important, loyalty to the administration. Still it could not be denied that he was a loose end. Nobody in Washington, Hunter reflected, was indispensable, not even Collins.

The National Security Adviser went over in his mind his options for handling the problem. He had resort to individuals on the White House staff cable to removing Collins, but that might be messy. It was better to avoid any direct links to the operation and his people might have a problem in concealing the fact that Collin's death was not murder.

Hunter decided that upon returning to his office, he would call a contact and have them arrange for foreign operatives to carry out the operation. He would arrange to hide the fact that the target individual was the American CIA Director. As they had on previous such missions, they would make Collin's demise look accidental and then leave the country immediately.

His problem resolved, Hunter left the club and walked down F Street toward his office in the Executive Office Building. Stopping at a corner for a traffic light he looked about him and smiled. It was a perfect day in this perfect world. How fortunate he was, he realized, to be living in as beautiful a city as Washington, DC and to simultaneously be able to serve his country.

THE RUSSIAN SPY-MASTER

Lieutenant Colonel Viktor Borin sat behind his desk in his office in the headquarters of the Main Intelligence Directorate of the General Staff (GRU). He was a short, squat, muscular man, only in his mid- forties, although he looked some ten years older. Borin owed his key post, Chief of U.S. Operations, not only to his considerable ability but also to the fact that his late father, General Borin, had had many friends in the GRU. This had helped him with his promotion during his early years in the service.

Borin closely examined the young man standing before him. The Colonel had studied the man's personnel folder and was familiar with all of the details. The man, Andreev Gorkov, stood in a pose of attention, his shoulders braced back, his arms at his side. He was twenty-three, and Nordic in appearance, with blond hair and blue eyes.

"What is your name?" Borin shouted in Russian.

Gorkov looked at him silently, saying nothing.

"Damn it!" Borin roared again in Russian, "What is your name? Are you too stupid to answer?"

The young man shook his head and smiled. "I don't understand you, sir" he said in English which conveyed no hint that he had been born and raised in Russia, "Is that Russian you're speaking?"

The Colonel smiled to himself. Gorkov had learned his lessons well. His behavior comported with the reports of his instructors that he was a perfect candidate for service as a long-term, deep-cover agent in the United States.

"All right," Borin said, speaking now in English which was almost as good as Gorkov's. Borin had not studied English at the GRU Academy as had Gorkov. Instead, the Colonel had acquired his fluency in the United States, first as a graduate student and subsequently at two tours there, in at the United Nations and subsequently as the Chief of the GRU station at the Embassy in Washington. "At ease. Please tell me about yourself."

Gorkov relaxed. "Sir, " he said, "My name is William Harvey. I was born in New York City and am twenty-three years old. I attended New York University, majoring in history. My father Paul died recently, leaving me a small amount of money. I love photography and plan to use my inheritance to start a small camera shop in Washington. Would you like any more details, sir?"

Bornin smiled. Gorkov knew his cover story well. The Colonel decided against pushing further. It really made no sense. As chief of U.S. operations, Borin theoretically had the power to reject any candidate for assignment to the United States. However, Gorkov had already been vetted and approved by General Rosovsky, Borin's direct superior and Chief of Operations in the Western Hemisphere.

Rosovsky reacted violently when any o f his actions was questioned, most particularly by a subordinate. The General's good will was essential if Borin was to receive his promotion to full colonel. Clearly, it would be stupid of him to find fault with Gorkov, particularly as the young man did seem to be competent. Instead, Borin asked his final question, "Are you married?"

"I am not at present."

It was the perfect answer. Borin smiled. Interviewing the GRU officers assigned to serve in the United States was the part of his job he liked best. The rest of it was the problem. Every time a GRU officer in the United States blundered, or even If one of their American agents made a mistake, Rosovsky held him personally responsible." Damn the General"! He thought. "May God strike him dead!"

Borin was surprised by his own anger. He was not a particularly religious man. He would have to watch his step, to be careful his antipathy to the General did not show. Rosovsky was a dangerous boss; he would be an even more dangerous enemy.

The Colonel had never before had a serious problem with a boss. He had gotten along well with General Petkov, Rosovsky's predecessor. Borin wondered if Rosovsky's antipathy toward him was based on the Generals lack of experience I clandestine operations and his suspicion Borin held him in low esteem.

In addition to his powerful position, the General was a childhood friend of the president; rumor had to that he and the President had been classmates and that Rosovsky had stepped in to save the future president from the school bully. Now, the General and the President went off together on hunting trips and whored at the President's mountain retreat.

The Colonel switched on his intercom and ordered his secretary "Send in the young woman."

A minute later a young woman entered and stood at attention next to Gorkov. "What is your name?" Borin demanded in Russian.

She started to respond and then caught herself. "I'm afraid I don't understand you," she said in fluent English. It was clear she was not as well trained as Gorkov, but that was no problem. Gorkov's job would be handling agents. Her job, if she went with him, was to purely as a support agent.

Gorkov looked relieved that she had answered properly. Borin understood this; it was hard not to like her. She was pretty, with a nice figure and a sweet face. Her jet black hair was tied in back with a bright ribbon. She was not the type the Colonel would have liked to go to bed with; she was what he would have wanted if he had had a daughter.

Boring realized that if his wife Olga had agreed to have children, their daughter would be about this girl's age. It was Olga's anger at his refusal to use her family's influence to transfer from the GRU to the diplomatic service that started their marriage going sour. Then had come her refusal to have children. By now, he could hardly stand the sight of her although they continued to live as husband and wife.

For at least the past year he had been certain that Olga was carrying on affairs behind his back. He frequently daydreamed of throwing her out of the house and divorcing her, but that would have been foolish. The GRU did not like to see their senior officers having marital difficulties – it could indicate personal weakness. Moreover, she came from a powerful family; her brother was a senior official in the Moscow mayor's office and a confidant of the president. He did not care much for Borin and would take a dim view of the Colonel's divorcing his sister. It was much wiser, he decided, to wait until he received his promotion to full Colonel before throwing her out.

Enough with this daydreaming, Borin thought, bringing himself back to the matter at hand. "What is your name?" he asked in English in a kinder tone.

"Anne Cartwright," she answered.

"Tell me about yourself."

She gave him the answers he expected. She had learned her cover story well. "Are you married?" he asked.

"No sir."

"One more thing," he said. "Both of you turn and look at each other carefully. As you probably surmise, the plan is to send you to the United States as husband and wife. On paper, you will be married. Whether you engage in marital relations is up to you, but to all outsiders you must behave like a loving couple. Can you handle that?"

"Yes, sir," they answered, almost in unison.

That was to be expected. The chance to live under deep cover in America was one most Russians would die for. The man or woman selected by the GRU as a prospective spouse would have to act and look like Medusa before a Russian would turn it down and risk the chance of losing the assignment to the United States. And both the man and the woman were bright, eager and well-spoken. Borin was sorry he had not been assigned such a wife before going on his first overseas assignment. That way, he would have escaped his present relation with Olga. But he had been sent in an official status to an embassy and had the mistaken impression that she would be a loving and faithful wife.

"Good," he told the couple. "You will be married here and then travel on a Russian freighter to Mexico. There you will land and assume your cover identities as Americans. When you leave this office, see Captain Zandorf. He will brief you on the details. Good Luck."

They saluted, thanked him and went out. Borin smiled to himself. They were a lovely young couple. In some way he envied Gorkov. It would be nice to be twenty-four again and setting out on an assignment in America with an attractive, affectionate wife. Perhaps he should have followed the example of his younger brother Alexi, who had rebelled against their father and refused to join the GRU. As a young man, Borin had been fascinated by history and had thought of teaching the subject at a university.

The Colonel thought about his life for a minute, then shook his head. This was foolish. Alexi was now a poorly-paid government clerk with a fat wife and two unpleasant children.

157

He lived in a dilapidated apartment building barely better than a slum.

Borin, by contrast, was a senior intelligence officer, earning a salary many times high than that of most Russians. He and Olga shared a large luxury apartment in the best apartment building in Moscow, one reserved for senior officials. He owned a new European sports car and could shop for luxury goods in the store open only to senior officials. Moreover, because of his job as head of American operations, he could have the GRU mission in Washington buy and ship to him anything in the United States he desired. His apartment contained many American books and magazines not available in Russia and for Olga, he had obtained a pair of the jeans widely sought after by Russian women.

Borin's reverie was broken. The door of his office was flung open, and General Rosovsky stormed in. The General's face was red with rage, the white scar on his cheek from a wound he had received fighting the Chechens, standing out. Waving a piece of paper, he shouted: "What's this about Star Man?".

Star Man was the code name of George Cartwright, the GRU's most valuable agent in the United States. For almost five years Star Man had provided high-level information on American political and military secrets. A senior official of the State Department, he had contacted the Russian Embassy in Mexico to offer his services in exchange for a large amount of cash. The colonel had handled him in Washington himself before moving up to head the GRU unit there. Despite the priceless information, Star Man provided, Borin had never liked or trusted him. Money was not particularly good leverage for controlling an agent, a feeling of dislike for America or sympathy for Russia would have been much better.

"Could I see that report, sir?" Borin asked politely. "This is the first I have heard of it."

Rosovsky thrust the paper into Borin's hand. The colonel read it quickly. It was an urgent message from Major Zhdanov, head of the GRU Station in Washington. It reported that Star Man had been arrested by the FBI during a meeting in Rock Creek Park in Washington with Captain Lavrov, his handler. Lvov had been questioned and released because of his diplomatic status; Star Man was still being held incommunicado.

This was serious. Star Man was by far the GRU's most valuable mole in the United States. A senior career official at the State Department,he had for almost five years provided the GRU with highly-classified information about American political and military affairs. Borin, himself, had been Star Man's case officer for a year before moving up to head the GRU station in Washington. The colonel had not recruited him, Star Man had volunteered his services in return for a large, regular cash payment. Star Man was the agent he had cared for least, finding the man pompous and arrogant.

Borin felt he had to say something. He struggled to find the right words. Rosovsky had only limited experience in dealing with agents. Whatever Borin said had to be something the General could understand and not set him off in a rage directed against him. He came up with, "They'll undoubtedly declare Lavrov PNG and ship him out of the country."

"I don't give a damn about Lavrov," Rosovsky shouted, "What do you propose to do about this mess?"

The colonel realized his peril. Rosovsky had the propensity of seeking a scapegoat whenever something bad happened. I made no difference whether the individual chosen was responsible or not, any convenient figure would do. The wisest thing for him to do, Borin realized, was to get as far away from the general as possible.

"I should leave at once for Washington." To investigate what went wrong," Borin said. "To find out whether the fault was Lavrov's or Star Man's. I also have to make sure Zhdanov had not failed to adhere to the security arrangements I established when I was head of the Washington unit."

"Is it convenient for you to leave your post at this time?" Rosovsky asked.

"No, sir, but it's necessary. We have to find out all the details about this mess and make sure it doesn't happen again. I won't be in Washington for more than a few days. I think Major Groshkin can handle things here well enough for the brief time I'll be gone.

This was a complete lie. Borin knew that Groshkin would foul things up. The man was too stupid to be able to paint an out-house. The colonel could have several weeks work once he returned home to clean up the damage caused by Groshkin's stupidity. The better choice to act for him during his trip would have been Major Malinov. But Malinov was ambitious.

He would take advantage of Borin's absence to insinuate himself with Rosovsky and undercut the colonel.

"All right," the General said. "How soon can you leave?"

"Right away," Borin answered. The sooner, the better. I'll go home to pick up a few things and take the next flight to Washington. Rosovsky said nothing more, turned and left. Borin breathed a sigh of relief. It had been a lucky escape. The General could very easily have fired him on the spot. There would have been no redress. The General was a favorite of Russia's President, the two frequently spending weekend's drinking and wenching at the Presidential dacha in the country.

The Colonel quickly took care of a few urgent matters, then summoned his staff and told them of his trip to Washington and Groshkin's acting for him. He saw out of the corner of his eye Malinov frowning at the news. Borin made a mental note to transfer Malinov to some remote foreign post at the next opportunity. You could say what you like about the wisdom of keeping your enemies near you, in this case, Malinov could do less harm far away that in the GRU headquarters.

Groshkin's briefing required no more than a few minutes. It made little sense to burden him with too much information; the man's intelligence was too limited for him to absorb much. God help the GRU, Borin thought, with officers like Groshkin moving up in the ranks. The Colonel then went downstairs and ordered his driver, Sergeant Turov, to take him home.

During the ride, Borin and the driver chatted amicably. The driver indicated his disappointment at learning that the colonel would be away from Moscow for a few days. During his absence, the driver would have to chauffeur other officers, and he considered himself fortunate in working as Borin's full-time driver. As long as a subordinate did a good job, the Colonel was cordial and polite to him.

Borin arrived at him apartment house and took the elevator to his floor. He entered his apartment and was surprised to find Olga there. Probably, he thought bitterly, she has finished with her afternoon lover and was dressing to see the evening one.

"Good afternoon," he said politely, giving her a pro forma kiss on the cheek. There was no reason to reveal to Olga the deep dislike he felt for her. He told her he would be leaving for a few days on a mission. She seemed pleased by the news. He hoped she would not entertain one of her lovers at the apartment during his absence. If she did and he became known publicly as a cuckolded husband, he decided, he would kick her out, regardless of the effect on his promotion.

The Colonel did not like to carry heavy luggage with him when he traveled. He packed just a few things that he would need in Washington in a small suitcase; if something required cleaning, he would get it done at the hotel or simply purchase a replacement. As he packed, he looked around the apartment, taking pride in its modern appliances: the Swedish refrigerator, the American electric oven, the Australian coffee maker.

Borin interrupted his packing to walk up to a large bookcase and take from behind the books on the top shelf his pistol. It was loaded, but with no bullet in the chamber. It was something he had learned from his father, who had survived the Stalinist purges. He recalled from his youth the elder Borin commenting that if they came to arrest him, he would take as many of them as he could with him.

Shouting goodbye to his wife, the Colonel descended in the elevator to the lobby, exited the building and had the militiaman standing in front summon a taxi to take him to the airport. Borin had left it to his secretary to arrange for the airline tickets, ordering her to take whichever air line was leaving Moscow first. After several calls, she had been successful in obtaining a seat for him on Aeroflot, although the flight had been filled, by stressing the importance of his trip for the GRU.

In past years, he would have preferred flying on an American airline; the Americans maintained their planes better than did the Russians and American pilots were better trained to handle emergencies. In recent years, however, he had chosen Aeroflot because of his concern over the flaws in American security procedures. They were so stupid about profiling that they did not do thorough checks of obviously suspicious passengers; it was a common joke in the GRU headquarters that an Islamic terrorist would have to be carrying a bomb with a lit fuse in his hands while passing through security before he would attract any attention.

Arriving at the airport, the colonel had sailed through customs and boarded the flight early. It soon filled, leaving

Borin unpleasantly crowded. Annoyed, he called over the stewardess, showed her is identification and requested a seat in the first class compartment, a demand with which she swiftly complied. Borin made a mental note to instruct his secretary to arrange all future travel for him in a first class section.

The flight to New York was reasonably pleasant, and after a change in planes, Borin arrived at Dulles Airport outside of Washington. The GRU Station had sent out a car and driver to meet him along with Lieutenant Nemtsov, a junior officer in the unit. Borin was pleased that the young officer had the intelligence not to salute him, realizing that he had no wish to draw attention to himself from any American officials who might be watching. Nemtsov's discretion was, unfortunately, not shared by Zhdanov, who had sent out an Embassy car with a diplomatic license plate which clearly identified to any U.S. government observer that it belonged to the Russian Embassy.

As the car drove left the airport, the Lieutenant explained that Zhdanov had arranged for Borin to stay at one of the Embassy guest houses in Washington. The Colonel was not surprised by this suggestion but had no intention of complying. Anyone who chose to stay at an Embassy guest house instead of in one of the American luxury hotels would have to be a fool."That won't be necessary," Borin interrupted him "Just drop me at DuPont Circle. I prefer to stay at one of the hotels on Massachusetts Avenue. Tell Major Zhdanov that I will be at the Embassy as soon as I have a chance to rest and wash up."

Nemtsov knew better than to argue. In response to his request, the car deposited him at DuPont Circle and Borin walked briskly to the hotel. He was well acquainted with Washington from his years of service in the capital. He checked in without difficulty, signing the register simply as Mr. Borin and giving as his address a made-up one in New York. The FBI probably knew about his arrival in Washington already, but there was no sense in making it easier for them if they did not.

The hotel room was as comfortable as Borin expected. You had to hand it to the Americans. They certainly knew how to run first class hotels. The Colonel washed up, made a cup of coffee using the coffee maker in his room and then went downstairs. The Russian Embassy was too far for Borin to walk, but it had the advantage of being closer to the center of town. The Colonel hailed a taxi and reached the embassy in a matter of minutes.

Arriving at the embassy, Borin paid the driver and walked past the American security guards lackadaisically guarding the building into the courtyard. Inside the embassy, he showed his identification to the Russian security officer and then ascended the staircase to the higher floor housing the GRU unit. The secretary who greeted him was not someone he recognized. "Good morning," he said in English, "I'm Colonel Borin. I'm here to see Major Zhdanov."

"Yes, sir," she said in Russian, jumping up from her desk and escorting him into the Major's office. She obviously had been alerted to treat him with deference. The first thing that struck him was that Zhdanov had redecorated it, replacing the

165

formal mahogany furniture he had used with a Swedish desk and bookcase. Mounted on the wall was the head of a Siberian tiger Zhdanov had shot. Borin shuddered, He didn't care for hunting; unless you were killing for food hunting seemed nothing more than a purposeless slaughter of living things.

"Good morning, sir," Zhdanov said, rising to greet him. "It's good to see you again." The man's smile was clearly forced; he was unable to conceal the fear he felt. He was well aware that if Borin held him responsible for the arrest of Star Man, it could result in the Major's replacement as GRU chief in Washington and possibly his firing from the service.

"Good morning, Major," Borin answered, keeping his tone neutral. It would be unfair to Zhdanov to show any emotion, any feeling of sympathy or anger until he ascertained all the facts in the case. "Please brief me on all of the details of star man's arrest."

Zhdanov swallowed hard. "We don't know how the FBI got wind of the meeting," he said. "We followed all the procedures."

This was the answer Borin expected. If he had faced the same predicament, he would have behaved similarly. Someone like General Rosovsky, of course, would have put all the blame on the case officer, Captain Lavrov. This was a point in Zhdanov's favor.

"Is Lavrov still in the U.S.?" Borin asked.

"Yes, sir. The FBI gave him seventy-two hours to leave the country. He is at home supervising the packing of his effects. I'll call to have him come here immediately."

166

"Good. Now, I'd like an office in which I can work and if you would have someone bring me Star Man's dossier. I'd like to read in on all the latest details."

"Yes, sir. "

Zhdanov showed the colonel to an empty office and instructed his secretary to bring the Star Man file to Borin. The earlier parts of the dossier were familiar to the Colonel from his time in Washington. He skimmed through them to refresh his memory and then carefully scrutinized the records following his departure from the Embassy. As he expected, there were flaws in the handling of the agent. This was inevitable; if all the recommended procedures were followed with every agent meeting, there would be no time to handle most of the work. Shortcuts had to be taken.

As he read, the Colonel made notes to use when he prepared the report of his investigation he would turn in to Rosovsky on his return to Moscow. Two facts stood out as important. The meeting at which Star Man had been arrested by the FBI took place at Rock Creek Park on a Wednesday night, as had three of the previous four meetings Lavrov had with the agent. Elemental trade=craft called for the timing of meetings with agents to vary as to time, place and day of the week to prevent a pattern becoming obvious to any possible surveillance. The second was the failure of Lavrov or any other GRU officer to arrive at the meeting spot early to check for any suspicious on-lookers.

Borin' s was interrupted by a knock at the office door, and Lavrov entered. He was a good-looking blond man in his mid-thirties. Borin and interviewed him in Moscow before approving his assignment to Washington and had been favorably impressed by his demeanor and obvious intelligence.

Lavrov saluted and said, "Good morning, sir. You wished to see me. "

"Yes," the Colonel answered in a quiet voice, "Please sit down and tell me about Star Man's arrest."

Lavrov proceeded to relate the details. Star Man had signaled he needed to see his case officer, the time, and place of a future meeting had been set at the previous one, and he had seen nothing suspicious when he approached the site in Rock Creek Park. The FBI apparently had somehow gotten wind of it and were staking out the spot from various locations, including a closed highways department repair van.

"Thank you, Captain," Borin said when Lavrov finished his account. " That was an excellent report. You can go home to resume your packing. Good luck."

Lavrov searched anxiously for some sign of what is fate would be, but could detect nothing from Borin's tone. "Yes, sir, thank you, sir," he said, saluting, and left.

The Colonel sat back after Lavrov's departure, pondering what he had learned thus far about Star Man's arrest. All things considered, the Captain and Zhdanov had acted in a professional manner, despite the errors in the procedure he had found. Star Man's arrest was just one of those things that had to be expected. Five years was a long time for an agent to provide the type of information Star Man had provided without being detected by American counter-intelligence.

This, however, was not something he could tell General Rosovsky. If he submitted a report with these finding the General would explode and blame him for the arrest. As much as he was loath to sacrifice Lavrov or Zhdanov, better their heads than his. Borin looked at his watch. It was already past three, and he was exhausted from the flight across the Atlantic and his study of the dossier. It was time to go back to his hotel and relax. He would review the situation tomorrow when his mind was fresh.

The Colonel stood took the Star Man file with him and brought it in to the secretary. Telling her he was going back to the hotel and would return tomorrow, he went downstairs and exited the embassy. He stood for a minute on Wisconsin Avenue enjoying the sun and then hailed a cab to take him to his hotel. Back in his room, he undressed, took a shower, and then curled up in the comfortable bed for a nap.

An hour later, Borin woke up refreshed. He dressed, then went downstairs to the lobby and asked the concierge to try and get him a ticket to a good play, preferably one at the Kennedy Center. The concierge was successful, and the Colonel went off happily to the Kennedy Center, which he had occasionally frequented during his tour in Washington.

After a quick meal in the Kennedy Center cafeteria, Borin entered the large theater. The play he saw turned out to be a musical on a road tour after its stint on Broadway. Borin had spent enough time in the U.S. to be thoroughly familiar with

American idioms customs and had had enjoyed going to Broadway shows when he was a student in New York. He enjoyed the dancing and settings of the play but found the modern music discordant to his ears. It was typical, he thought, of the way American culture had deteriorated over the years.

Back at the hotel, the Colonel relaxed in bed think about the day. It was pleasant to be back in Washington, although he would have preferred the circumstances to be different. When he found his thoughts turning to the Star Man affair and how to deal with it, he forced the thought out of his mind and turned off the light.

The next morning Borin slept late. Awakening, he shaved, dressed and went downstairs where he enjoyed the complimentary breakfast buffet in the hotel dining room. He then took his suitcase, checked out of the hotel and went out onto the street, looking around for a taxi to take him to the Embassy.

"Victor," he heard a familiar voice say behind him. Surprised, He spun around and found himself facing a man in a business suit, about his own height and wearing a hat and sunglasses. For a moment he didn't recognize the man, then he suddenly realized who it was. "Jim," he said smiling, "Jim MacDonald."

He had met MacDonald in New York about five years ago, at a United Nations cocktail party. The two had been standing next to each other at the canape table and had exchanged polite remarks. When it turned out that both of them were diplomats and liked Smorgasbord buffets, they had arranged to meet at a well-known New York Smorgasbord restaurant the following week.

Each man quickly suspected that the other was an intelligence officer, although Borin was not sure if MacDonald was CIA or FBI. MacDonald managed to include in his conversation discrete questions bout the Colonel's upbringing and family, which Borin recognized as standard procedure in assessing the vulnerability of a potential agent. Borin, in turn, did the same. After several lunches, the two men realized that they were each an experienced professional intelligence officer and that neither had the slightest thought of defecting to the other side.

Nonetheless, they enjoyed their friendship and continued meeting. From time to time they helped each other out. While neither would reveal sensitive information about their own country, they exchanged useful tidbits about third countries. MacDonald had helped him out with some information on Chinese policy toward Vietnam; he had repaid the favor by giving MacDonald information on Israel's attitude toward Syria.

"What a surprise to see you here in Washington," MacDonald said, smiling and shaking the Colonel's hand. "You look great."

"So do you, Jim," Borin answered, returning the compliment." There was no doubt in the Colonel's mind that MacDonald was happy to see him. However, he was even more sure that their meeting was no accident. The American had planned it for some reason. Borin waited to learn what it was.

"Can I give you a lift somewhere?" MacDonald asked, "That's my car over there," he said, pointing to a large black one parked in front of the hotel. Borin looked and noticed it was in a no-parking zone. Apparently the American intelligence officers enjoyed the same clout the GRU did in Russia.

"No, thanks, Jim. I'm on my way to the Russian Embassy, and they might get the wrong idea if they saw me getting out of your car."

"Don't worry," MacDonald said, taking the Colonel's arm and steering him to the car. "I'll drop you on Wisconsin Avenue, and you can walk or take a cab the last part of the way."

Borin was curious about what MacDonald was up to and acquiesced. As they drove off, the American turned to look at Borin. " Actually, MacDonald admitted, "When we caught Cartwright, I thought you'd to come to Washington to look into the matter. Knowing you and knowing that you are head of American operations, it was an easy thing to predict."

The Colonel was not surprised that American intelligence was aware of his position. They undoubtedly had their own agents in Moscow. He said nothing, not wishing to either affirm or deny MacDonald's words. "Cartwright, by the way," MacDonald continued, "Is singing like a canary. He is scared shitless at the thought of spending the rest of his life in a federal prison and leaped at the prospect we might show him

172

some leniency if he talked. He mentioned that you were one of his case officers in Washington."

Borin still said nothing. MacDonald waited for a minute, then continued. "I have to tell you I am surprised by the lack of compartmentalization at your Embassy. He not only told as everything he has given you but also identified three other Russian agents here in Washington, Peter Starbuck, Louis Moore, and Anthony Turner."

"This was a catastrophe," Borin thought, as he struggled to keep his concern from showing. It Starbuck, Moore, and Goldberg, along with Cartwright, were the most important Russian agents in America. Their arrest would wipe out the GRU's ability to monitor American government security policy and activities."

The Colonel continued to say nothing. MacDonald went on," We were going to arrest Starbuck, Moore and Turner as soon as Cartwright identified them, but decided to hold up. I hate to do this to you, but we thought we'd gain more by delaying picking them up until you came here. When we arrest them now, while you're in Washington, you can hardly escape being blamed for the arrests. When you go back to Moscow, I think your reception will be on the frosty side. If they don't fire your form the service, you'll probably end up sitting in an office the size of a broom closet, staring at obsolete files. "

Borin couldn't help but smile at the picture MacDonald was painting. The American's prediction was probably close to the truth. "It's nothing like that at all, the Colonel answered.

'You know my people are just as loving and forgiving as yours."

It was MacDonald's turn to smile. "That's just what I mean," he said. "Look, Jim," he went on, "Why don't you stay here and work for us. You'll be well treated. You really don't have a future in the GRU any more. You once told me that as a young man, you wanted to be a history professor. We can arrange things, so you do that here. It would be easy for you to adjust. Hell, you've spent so much time in the US that you think like an American."

For a few seconds, the Colonel was tempted. It would be wonderful to get away from General Rosovsky, to longer have to worry about who Olga was sleeping with, to actually be a history professor. Then Borin smiled ruefully. "No," he said, "Though it's a tempting offer. But it just wouldn't work. I like being a GRU Colonel. I have power, prestige, a high salary and a lovely apartment. When I tell people to jump, they ask how high."

"That's all fine now, but will that continue after you return to Moscow?" MacDonald asked seriously. "I don't see how you can expect to escape being blamed for the arrests here."

"It may be awkward for a bit, but I doubt they will bounce me," Borin said, sounding more confident than he felt. And if I stayed here," he added, what sort of future would I have. You'd question me in a safe house for a couple of months till you extracted all the information I had. Then you'd give me a false identity and resettle me someplace far from Washington, probably set me up in a small business to support myself. I really can't see myself living in Peoria and running a used book shop there. "

The American laughed. "That's a pretty dismal picture you're painting. It would be better than that. We might be able to have you lecture at our intelligence training facility. Possibly even at a private college or university."

"No," the Colonel came back. "If I taught under my own name I'd be a sitting duck for a GRU assassin and if I was in alias no college would use me." Thinking quickly, he added "I have a better idea. Suppose you don't arrest Starbuck, Moore and Turner. If you suspect them of being moles, you cut off their access to sensitive materials. They would be very useful to you as a channel for disseminating disinformation to Moscow."

"That would certainly help you out," MacDonald said, "But what would we get out of it. I"d like to assist you, but my superiors would never swallow such an arrangement."

"There's more," Borin came back quickly. "I can get you a high-level asset in Moscow. One who knows all the Russian's intelligence operations."

The American's jaw dropped. "Are you offering to work for us?"

"Under the right conditions," Borin began slowly. " I am here to investigate Cartwright's arrest and to write up a report of my findings. I have two choices. First, I can conclude that his arrest, or that of all four of them, was the result of poor handling and trade-craft by the Station Officer. That probably will get me off the hook. "

"On the other hand," he continued, " I can find that everything in Washington was handled in a first-class manner. I can add that Cartwright's arrest might have been the result of information provided by a high-level American penetration of the GRU in Moscow. My superior, General Rosovsky, will become the object of suspicion.".

MacDonald smiled wryly. "So you want to use us to get rid of your boss? I can see how you'd profit, but what use would that be to us? You're not suggesting that you'd become an American agent, are you? I'd find that very hard to believe."

"Of course not," Borin answered. "I 'm a loyal Russian. I have no more interest in becoming an American spy that you have in becoming a Russian one. I said I would secure you an asset, not an agent."

"Just what's the difference?"

"You mentioned that I'm half-American. That's true. I've spent so much time studying and working here that I think like an American. I know America far better than most of my government, particularly the President and his associates. I know that the U.S. is not always plotting to destroy or humble Russia. If I replace Rosovsky as Chief of Western Hemisphere Operations, I'll be in a good position to solve a lot of the problems that come up between our two countries.

"Is that all you want?"

"No," said Borin. He was thinking carefully, seeking desperately to rescue himself from the mess he was in. He knew his future in the GRU and possibly his entire life rested upon his ability to convince the American of his sincerity. "My report implicating Rosovsky may not be enough. I'd need to to use your agents in Moscow to spread rumors that the General is an American agent."

MacDonald shook his head. "All that's above my pay grade. I'll have to run that past my superiors to see if they'd buy such a deal."

"Understood. I don't think it would be a good idea for us to meet again in public. I'm leaving this afternoon for Moscow on Aeroflot. If your superiors approve the arrangement, have someone leave a package addressed to me at the airline desk. The package should contain a movie disc, say one of James Bond's movies. I'll understand that as the sign for me to deliver my report along the lines we've discussed."

As they drove north toward the Russian Embassy, Borin glanced sideways at MacDonald, hoping to gather from the American' s expression whether his pitch had been successful. It was impossible to tell. Borin relaxed. He had tried his best. He could do no more. A few minutes later, MacDonald pulled over to the curb and stopped. "We're a few blocks from the Embassy," he said. "I'd better let you out here. I'll check with my superiors and let you know if they agree by sending the tape to you at the Aeroflot desk. They shook hands and Borin climbed out of the car, suitcase in hand. Waving back, he walked slowly to the Embassy, his mind racing.

The Colonel strode into the Embassy, passing the Russian security guards who did not stop him. As he returned their salute, he smiled to himself. Obviously, Major Zhdanov had passed the word to the Embassy personnel to treat him carefully. Ascending the staircase, he reached the floor housing the GRU unit and obtained from the secretary the folder he had left with her the previous day containing the files on Star Man.

Seating himself in the office Zhdanov had given him for his use, Borin carefully re-read the files. He then began to compose his report. The Colonel was a skilled drafter, and the words came easily. He summarized the details of Star Man's arrest by the FBI and of the security precautions Captain Lavrov and Major Zhdanov had employed. The overwhelming weight of the evidence, he concluded, indicated that the GRU staff in Washington had conducted themselves in an exemplary manner. The most probable cause of the agent's arrest was a leak from about the operation somewhere else, probably in Moscow.

Borin did not bother to list the names of the possible suspects. There was no need. Not more than a half-dozen people in the GRU knew the details of the Star Man operation. As one of these, General Rosovsky could easily fall under suspicion. Now, if the American agents in Moscow spread the story Rosovsky was the American mole, Borin would be well on his way to replacing him.

When he had finished his report and reviewed it, the Colonel personally encrypted it, the placed the document in his jacket pocket. He thought for a few minutes, then began drafting a second version of his findings. He carefully detailed all the flaws he had found in the Washington GRU's handling of Star Man, stressing that the security procedures he had initiated concerning the handling of sensitive agents had been repeated ignored. He concluded the report with the recommendation that Major Zhdanov and Captain Lavrov receive formal reprimands for their infractions and be reassigned to Moscow as soon as suitable replacements could be obtained. Borin then encrypted this version and placed it in his jacket pocket along with the other.

Making Zhdanov and Lavrov the fall guys for the agent's arrest was not something Borin enjoyed doing. Hopefully, he would not have to submit this version. Still, it was better to sacrifice their necks than his own. And, if in the future he might safely be able to rehabilitate them, he would do so.

The Colonel reassembled the Sky Man file, checked the desk to make sure he had left no classified materials in it, then returned the folder to Zhdanov's secretary. Both the dictates of politeness and protocol required him now to say goodbye to Zhdanov and to thank him for his assistance. However, he couldn't bring himself to face the Major and to act as though everything was fine. "Please thank the Major for his aid," he told the secretary, "And tell him I'm leaving for the airport to return to Moscow." Without waiting for her reply, he fled.

Although it was only early afternoon, Borin felt fatigued from the day's events. Normally, he would have taken advantage of his time in Washington to visit a museum or eat in a fine restaurant. Instead, upon leaving the Embassy, he hailed a cab and had it take him directly to Dulles Airport. At the Aeroflot counter, he was surprised and disappointed to find there was no direct flight back to Moscow until the following morning. The desk clerk informed him that he would have to take a flight to New York's Kennedy Airport and board a flight for Moscow there.

Rather than delay his departure, the Colonel checked his bags through and picked up the tickets. Although he would have to travel by way of New York, at least the leg from New York to Moscow was in first-class.

Asking the counter agent if there was a package left for him, Borin received a negative response. This was disappointing but not unexpected. He shrugged his shoulders and went off to get a quick sandwich at a stand and to buy that day's edition of the "New York Times" to read on the plane.

When he heard his plane's loading announcement, Borin headed to the departure gate. As he showed his ticket to the attendant, she confirmed that he was Mr. Borin and then handed him a small package addressed to him. There was no identification of the sender, but the Colonel needed none. It had to be from MacDonald, signaling him that his proposal had been accepted. Boring ripped open the package. It contained the James Bond movie he had requested.

The flight to New York went smoothly. Borin found the Kennedy Airport even more crowded than he remembered. He was relieved to board the Aeroflot plane to Moscow and settle in comfortably in his seat in the first class compartment. As he relaxed, enjoying the leg room and the quiet atmosphere, the stewardess came over and asked him in Russian if he would like a drink. Very likely, he thought, she was aware of his GRU status.

The Colonel enjoyed the dinner when it arrived. He skimmed the newspaper he had brought with him and attempted to divert himself with the movie being shown, but it was of no use. His mind kept on turning to the agreement he had reached with MacDonald and the two versions of the report he had prepared. If he submitted the one casting suspicion on Rosovsky, he could not turn it in to the General. The latter would simply rip it up and order him arrested.

Borin could go over Rosovsky's head and give his report directly to General Oleg, the head of the GRU, The Colonel had sufficient seniority to have direct access to Oleg . Possibly the latter might be interested in having an excuse to remove Rosovsky, whose ties with the President made him a potentially dangerous rival to head the GRU. On the other hand, Oleg would be reluctant to risk his neck by challenging Rosovsky. Borin realized, that if he were Oleg, he probably would hand the report to Rosovsky and let him deal with it.

The Colonel made his decision. He stood up and headed to the rest room. Locking the door, he extracted from his pocket a document, checking it to make sure it was the version of his report blaming Rosovsky for the leak leading to the arrest of Sky Man. Borin took out his cigarette lighter, a gift from Olga who had given it to him one Christmas, ignoring the fact that he didn't smoke. He lit it, applied the flame to the document. When most if the paper had burned, he put it into the wash and waited for the remainder to be consumed. He then carefully crumbled the ashes and washed the residue down the drain.

Returning to his seat, the Colonel reassured himself that he had made the right decision. If MacDonald's agents in Moscow were successful in casting suspicion on Rosovsky, the General could well be removed. Even the President would be unlikely to back him if it appeared he was an American mole. And if Borin was promoted to replace Rosovsky, the Colonel would help ease differences between his country and the United States as he had promised.

His decision made, the Colonel relaxed and dozed in his seat until breakfast was served. As he ate, he enjoyed looking at the scenery below him. The plane descended slowly and touched down gently, taxing to the arrival gate. Boring disembarked with the other first class passengers and was quickly passed through immigration control as soon as the inspector looked at his passport.

Looking at his watch, Borin saw that it was a little past eight in the morning. He decided he had time to stop off at his apartment to wash up and change before going on to the office; there was nothing he wished to add to his report and General Rosovsky was unlikely to arrive until well past nine. If the General had spent the previous night drinking with the President, he would likely be suffering a hangover and be in a nasty mood. Better, Borin thought, to give him time to sober up.

The taxi dropped the Colonel off at his apartment building. Receiving a salute from the militiaman on guard outside, he entered and took the elevator up to his floor. He found the apartment empty. Olga normally awakened late and should have been there if she had slept in the apartment that night. Clearly, she had not expected him back this soon and had spent the night with one of her lovers. The damn bitch, he said to himself.

With an effort, Borin turned his mind away from his adulterous wife. He had to have a clear head to deal with Rosovsky this morning. Calling his office to arrange for his driver to pick him up, he rapidly washed and changed his clothes. To escape from the apartment and the thoughts it evoked of his wife, Borin went downstairs and stood outside the building, waiting for his driver.

When the car arrived, the Colonel noted that it had been freshly washed and waxed. He climbed inside and said good morning to the Sergeant Turov. "Good morning, Colonel," the driver responded, "It's good to have you back." Turov's obvious sincerity as he spoke warmed Borin's heart. He felt a good officer should be liked and respected by his subordinates.

"Anything new?" Borin asked.

"Yes, sir. " the driver answered despondently, "The head of the motor pool took away my stripes. Claimed one of the officers I drove had been kept waiting for half an hour for me to pick him up. I tried to explain that I was stuck in traffic, but he wouldn't believe me."

"I'm sorry to hear that, the Colonel said thoughtfully. "I'll look into it."

Borin realized that Turov's waxing of the car had been designed to win his assistance in getting his sergeant's rank back. Still, Turov was a reliable chauffeur and as close to a friend as he might expect, given the differences in their rank. He decided to intervene in the matter.

The rode on in silence until the car arrived at the GRU Headquarters and the Colonel got out. Entering the building, he walked directly to the motor pool office and into the office of the dispatcher. The latter looked up surprised. He knew who Borin was but had never spoken to him before; like most users of the motor pool cars, arrangements for the Colonel's use of his car were handled by one of his subordinates.

"Don't you know enough to stand up when a Colonel enters the room?" Borin barked, his anger obvious. "

"I'm sorry, sir," the dispatcher said, jumping to attention and saluting. "I was so busy writing I wasn't aware of your presence."

"What's this about your demoting my driver without first checking with me? " Borin demanded. He rarely let his anger show, but now he was allowing it full rein.

"I'm terribly sorry, sir," the dispatcher said, trying to appease Borin. "You were out of the country, and Colonel Pulog complained that Turov had kept him waiting and then been disrespectful."

The Colonel knew Pulog and had no liking or respect for the man. More important, he was not an intelligence officer but in finance, no one Borin had to defer to. "You will restore

Turov to the rank of sergeant immediately. If Colonel Pulog doesn't like it, tell him to see me about it."

The Colonel turned and walked out, not waiting for the dispatcher's reply. The encounter left Borin feeling pleased. He genuinely preferred being nice to people, and it would be pleasant when Turov expressed his gratitude about the restoration of his sergeant's stripes. Hopefully, this would help to balance the damage he had done to Lavrov and Zhdanov when he placed the full responsibility on them for Star man's arrest.

Before going up to his office, Borin detoured to the snack bar and ordered a cup of coffee. As he left the snack bar, he passed a good looking young woman who smiled at him and said: "Welcome back Colonel, I hope your trip to Washington was successful."

Startled, Borin stopped in his tracks and turned around. How the Hell, he wondered, did this woman know about his mission to Washington. The entire affair was classified as most sensitive, with only a few officials in the GRU Headquarters privy to it.

He looked at her carefully. She appeared to be in her early twenties and exceptionally pretty. The tight clothes she wore accentuated her figure and her white blouse was open at the neck revealing a glimpse of cleavage. Borin was about to rebuke her for not saluting him but was dissuaded by her warm smile. "I'm afraid I don't know your name," said, his words sounding more austere than he intended."

"Kolchenka, sir," she answered, "Lieutenant EKaterina Kolchenka."

Borin had not seen her before and assumed she was newly assigned to the Headquarters. "What section are you in?" he asked, smiling. He enjoyed chatting with attractive women, and the Lieutenant's friendly demeanor was a pleasant change from dealing with Olga.

"The file room. Sir. I've been there for the last seven months."

So that explained it. The personnel in the file room occupied their own little world and rarely left it. Generally, new recruits not deemed worthy of foreign assignments were sent there and only those who showed exceptional ability allowed to escape.

"How do you like it?" he asked, prepared to offer some words of sympathy and encouragement.

Her response was unexpected: "It gives me the opportunity to read the personnel files carefully and to learn which agent handling techniques are the most successful."

Borin smiled in spite of himself. "You're interested in agent handling?"

"Yes, sir, particularly on a foreign assignment."

The Colonel found himself wondering if this chance encounter might prove useful. "I'll be occupied for a bit dealing with my trip to Washington, but when I have time, I'll call you. I might be able to give you some pointers on agent handling."

"I'd be very grateful, sir if you could."

She saluted and headed back to the file room. Borin stood admiring her figure until she turned into her office. He then ascended the staircase to his third-floor office.

Entering his office, the Colonel found Major Groshkin seated behind his desk, writing furiously. The Major jumped to his feet as soon as he saw his superior and saluted. "Welcome back, sir," he said.

"How is everything going? Borin asked, trying to conceal his apprehension. "No problems?"

The Colonel prayed that he would hear of no more arrests of his agents in Washington or of some impossible demand from Rosovsky. Borin let out a sigh of relief when Groshkin said, "Nothing of any importance, sir." He was about to ask Groshkin about Rosovsky's state of mind but decided it would be inappropriate; no need to permit his subordinate to become aware of his concern about the General. Instead, he informed the Major he would return shortly and went upstairs to Rosovsky's office.

Entering, Borin saluted smartly and said "Good morning General, I just got in from Washington and thought you'd like to receive my report immediately."

Rosovsky glared at him, his eyes bloodshot, a sullen expression his face. "Why the Hell didn't you send me some news from Washington? What were you trying to hide?"

The Colonel realized that the General was in a nasty mood and that he was about to receive the full force of his superior's anger. He interrupted Rosovsky, something he normally would not have done, in order to prevent the General from taking some rash action against him. Once Rosovsky said anything, he would be obdurate about amending his decision, regardless of the consequences.

I did not communicate to you while I was in Washington, "Borin said, because of the sensitivity of the matter. I knew you would not wish me to compromise security. While our code clerks are thoroughly indoctrinated on the need for security, they can be tempted to discuss really juicy gossip."

Rosovsky's attitude changed abruptly. Borin was highly regarded in the GRU as an expert agent handler. It would not be wise to challenge him on any matters of operational security. Even the General's powerful friends would shrink back from such a controversy. "Quite so," he said. "Give me your report."

"It's still encrypted, sir," the Colonel said. "I will decode it and give it to you, but I thought you'd like to receive an oral summary of my findings.

Rosovsky nodded in agreement.

"I regret to say I found the security situation at the Washington Station deplorable," Borin began. "The procedures I had established before I left have been permitted to lapse. This was particularly true in the meetings with Star Man and other very sensitive assets. The responsibility for this rests equally on Captain Lavrov and Major Zhdanov. There is a serious risk that other of our agents in Washington are under suspicion by the FBI and may also be arrested. I recommend that Lavrov and Zhdanov each receive formal reprimands and that they b transferred back here for a thorough review of their careers as soon as suitable replacements for them can be found."

As he said this, the Colonel reflected he was effectively ending the career of the two unfortunate officers. It was something he regretted, but he simply had no choice. It was either his neck or theirs. Hopefully, if the Americans succeeded in casting doubts about Rosovsky's loyalty and Borin replaced him, he would be able to correct the injustice by rehabilitating them.

Rosovsky listened to Borin's report in silence. When the latter had finished, Rosovsky coldly said, "You realize Colonel that as their superior and the officer in direct charge of supervising operations in Washington, you bear equal responsibility for Star Man's arrest."

This was a dangerous development and Borin realized he had to react decisively. "Let me remind you, sir," he said smoothly,"That in my report to you last month, I informed you I feared that security in Washington had become too lax and that corrective action should be taken. Since I do not have the authority to take such action without your approval, I was naturally awaiting your decision. If you wish, I will get a copy of my report out of the files to send you."

Borin was not actually lying, his report had contained the standard boiler-plate he inserted in such report to protect himself in case of a problem arising. In any case, Rosovsky did not call his bluff. The General's demeanor abruptly changed, and he smiled. "You misunderstand me, Colonel," he said. I hope you did not think I was implying any culpability on your part."

"Of course not, sir. If that's all, I'll return to my office and decode my report for you. I'll also start looking through the files for replacements for Lavrov and Zhdanov."

Borin saluted and returned to his office. He prepared the formal report to the General, revising some of the languages to buttress his conclusions. He then placed it in an envelope, sealed the envelopment and instructed his secretary to place it directly in Rosovsky's hands.

After his secretary had left, the Colonel sat back and thought about his situation. His report, he believed, would buy him some time. However, if Rosovsky remained on as his superior for any length of time or if there were more of his agents in Washington were arrested, his position would be in serious jeopardy. If both occurred, he would be fortunate to serve out the rest of his career as a Lieutenant Colonel running a file room in some remote part of Russia.

In any case, there was nothing more Borin could do; the situation was out of his hands. To calm his mind, he methodically went through the traffic that had been sent or received by his office while he was away. He found he had to correct several mistakes made by Groshkin, fortunately, only two were really serious ones. He corrected these and decided to correct the others later.

His immediate tasks completed, Borin thought about starting the job of obtaining replacements for Zhdanov and

Lavrov. However, his mind wasn't in it, and he decided to put it off until the next day. Looking at his watch, he saw that it was well past three. No wonder that he was feeling tired and hungry; the time change crossing the Atlantic and his failure to have a meal since breakfast on the plane were having a toll.

He thought about going home, but the idea of having to deal with Olga depressed him. Borin found himself thinking of Lieutenant Kolchenka. She was a beautiful woman, a girl really. It would be wonderful returning home and finding Ekaterina rather than Olga awaiting him.

The phone rang. Borin picked it up, and his secretary told him that it was his wife. "Viktor," she said when he picked it up. The militiaman informed me you had arrived home."

Not even a welcome or how are you," he thought bitterly. The coolness in her voice was obvious. "I was calling yo tell you," she added before he could say anything, "That I'm not going to be home tonight. My brother has an extra ticket to the ballet, so I'll go with them. Rather than come home so late, I'll spend the night with them."

The Colonel saw no purpose in objecting. In a way, he was relieved. Let whichever of her lovers she was sleeping with put up with her behavior.

Borin recalled the offer he had made to Lieutenant Kolchenka to call when he had some time. It had been an off-hand offer, and he had had no serious intention of actually doing so. Now, he changed his mind. Picking up the phone, he asked the operator to get him the file room.

When Ekaterina got on the line," he told her he had a few minutes to spare and that if she wished, she could come up to his office for a chat."

"That's awfully kind of you, sir," she said, "I'd love the opportunity." Her voice was sweet to his ears. "Perhaps," she suggested, "You might prefer to come over to my place after work. My room-mate is away so that it would be more private than talking to your office. If you're hungry, I'd be happy to fix you something to eat. We could meet outside the building at six o'clock."

The Colonel wondered if she was suggesting a romantic tete-a-tete. It certainly seemed like that to him.

"Why yes, "he said, "That would be lovely."

When he hung up," Borin sat back in his chair reflecting. With Olga away, there would be no problem in his spending the night with Ekaterina, if it turned out that way. Despite the failure of his marriage, he had no engaged in any extra-marital activity. Now, the restraints that had held him back were gone.

The General could hardly be nastier to him than he was already, whether or not he learned of Borin having an affair with the Lieutenant. The same was equally true of Olga. And if Rosovsky remained his superior, Borin's career was finished. Divorcing Olga would not harm it further.

The Colonel now considered the slim chance that he might replace a disgraced Rosovsky. Plenty of senior officials shed their_spouses and replaced them with attractive young women. He could do so too. He wondered if the Lieutenant was looking upon him as a possible mentor, was attracted to him or was simply hoping to trade her sexual favors for an assignment in Washington.

Borin decided her motivation made no difference to him. She was clearly intelligent and competent. She probably would be good at agent handling. There was no good reason why for a night in bed with her, he shouldn't approve an assignment for her to the Washington Station. He was surprised to find himself whistling. Life, he said to himself, can be pleasant after all.

CPSIA information can be obtained
at www.ICGtesting.com
Printed in the USA
LVOW10*1558030317
526088LV00005B/31/P